PENTHESILEA

PENTHESILEA

A TRAGIC DRAMA

HEINRICH VON KLEIST

Translated and Introduced by

JOEL AGEE

Pictures by

MAURICE SENDAK

Perennial

An Imprint of HarperCollins *Publishers*

To the memory of ALMA NEUMAN

J.A.

TRANSLATOR'S ACKNOWLEDGMENTS

I wish to thank the Simon R. Guggenheim Memorial Foundation and the Center Stage Theater of Baltimore for their financial aid. I am also obliged to the Corporation of Yaddo for a month's residence in quiet seclusion while I was working on this book.

Peter Demetz, Walter Arndt, and Paul Becker lent me invaluable assistance by reading and commenting on early drafts of the opening scenes. I am grateful as well to Lola Gruenthal, who carefully compared my finished version with the original and helped to improve it in numerous details.

I owe a special debt of gratitude to Mona Heinze for supporting this project from the beginning, and for the knowledge and love of Kleist's play she brought to her reading of its translation.

J . A .

CONTENTS

1

An army of one-breasted women sets out to conquer Greek heroes for the purpose of stocking their women's state with new female offspring. They blast into the midst of the Trojan War, confusing Greeks and Trojans alike and for a moment forcing those enemies into a terrified alliance. Achilles, the pride and mainstay of the Greeks, semidivine through his mother, a water nymph whose lineage goes back to Apollo, casts his eye on Penthesilea, Queen of the Amazons, herself a daughter of Ares, as she casts her eye on him. A chase begins,

> *The like of which not even the wildest storms*
> *Set loose to thunder across the plain of heaven*
> *Have yet presented to the astonished world,*

and it is the Queen who is hunting Achilles, to the uncomprehending horror of the Greeks. The tides of this private battle turn and return with mounting intensity, a whirl of erotic and martial obsession, elated, wild, relentless, making havoc of every gain the Greeks and the Amazons have made in their separate, perfectly rational campaigns. The fictional place is a field outside Troy, but the actual one, improbably, is a stage, and this orgy of constantly rekindled desire and frustration is played out within the metric strictures of blank verse—a tour de force of language that, in the words of one commentator, succeeds in "combining the extremes of sobriety and frenzy."

Such a theme, and such a treatment, could only offend sensibilities schooled in the idealizing Hellenism propounded by Herder and Winckelmann and practiced by Goethe, Schiller, and other German writers at the turn of the eighteenth to the nineteenth century. Still, if Kleist had been merely flirting with scandal, he might have given his story a comedic twist and gotten away with it. But the energy driving the amorous chase is tragic, and not merely in the thinned-out latter-day sense that makes the word more or less synonymous with "sad," but closer to the archaic roots of tragic theater than Kleist's contemporaries were prepared to countenance or than most of us, for that matter, can comfortably support. It is easier to laugh, as Goethe did, at the absurdity of a woman who has lost one breast assuring her lover that all her feelings have found refuge in her remaining breast than to follow her into a region where feeling manifests itself in material form and figures of speech become literally real, where death and love are identical twins and a murderous bite was only meant to be a kiss. Not that we are not acquainted with that place. A century after *Penthesilea* was written, Sigmund Freud rediscovered this teeming and uncanny world of unreason as an element into which we all descend every night of our lives, and which floods our waking consciousness at moments of passion and emotional confusion, sometimes with disastrous consequences.

2

"An unutterable human being," Kleist called himself—*"ein unaussprechlicher Mensch."* From a man who knows how to express himself, this is a peculiar phrase. There is a terrible literalness about it—as if he were baffled by the inevitable difference between words and what they refer to; as if he wanted to utter himself, literally, in his entirety, once and for all, instead of approximately and by indirection, like the rest of us. What sort of language would permit such immediate expression? It would have to be something like what Jakob Boehme called "the sensuous language of the birds and the beasts," which the souls of the blessed will speak at the end of time. Or the language of God, which lets there be light by the mere act of saying so. We are all unutterable, someone should have told him.

But Kleist knew this, and said as much in a celebrated essay titled "On the Marionette Theater," in which a famous dancer expatiates on the mysterious grace with which a puppet on its strings outdances all human competitors, even the greatest of whom are hobbled by self-consciousness. His interlocutor, a slightly distracted young man, responds by telling the dancer about an acquaintance, a beautiful youth whose attractiveness began to deteriorate from the moment when he recognized, in a mirror, his resemblance to a Greek statue and, fatefully, *aimed* at resembling it. The dancer then tells a story about a captive bear who was able to parry the lunges and thrusts of the most expert swordsman with an effortless flick of a paw. These images of unconscious genius and the sad deficiencies of acquired skill are adduced by Kleist in the service of an argument, more precisely a strategy, for the conquest of Paradise. Since, in the "organic" world, grace is most radiant and most commanding where reflection is darkest and weakest, and since an angel bars us from returning to Eden, it follows that we who are cursed with knowledge cannot regain our innocence except by going forward, around the world, as it were, driving reflection to its ultimate limit and beyond—"through an infinity"—until, graced with the consciousness of a god, we reenter Paradise by a back door and eat again of the forbidden fruit. Then we, too, will be capable of artless art, like the bear or the marionettes, or the beautiful youth before he tried to enact a perfection of being which he already possessed.

Such heaven-storming hubris could not go unavenged. Often in society, where formal composure and eloquent self-presentation could be as important as the style and fit of one's clothes, Kleist would be overcome by an uncontrollable tremor of the upper lip, or else he would blush and stammer. These somatic invasions were a torment. It seemed better to leave, to be alone. But the conversation would turn to subjects that mattered to him. Impulsively, he would join in—not always to converse or opine, but often to plunge into the unknown. His discourse, when he caught fire, was by all accounts dazzling. But then he would fall silent, his eyes would unfocus. He had abandoned his listeners for the company of his own thoughts. His lips moved, he mumbled. Embarrassed, the others would turn away and resume their conversation.

One day an author of great renown, Christoph Martin Wieland, at whose house Kleist was staying as a guest, asked him what he was muttering under his breath. Kleist reluctantly confessed that he was working on a tragedy which he was unable to commit to paper, because what he wrote always fell so far short of his ideal that he had no choice but to burn it. After much coaxing and pleading, he agreed to recite from memory a few grievously imperfect scenes from *Robert Guiskard, Duke of the Normans.* The older man described his impression in a letter to a friend:

> *I confess to you that I was astonished, and I do not believe I am saying too much when I assure you: If the spirits of Aeschylus, Sophocles, and Shakespeare had come together to write a tragedy, it would be Kleist's Death of Guiskard the Norman, provided the whole of it corresponded to what he allowed me to hear on that day.*

A few months later Kleist wrote to his sister Ulrike, from the northern French seaport of Saint-Omer, that he had abandoned his play as a task that exceeded his powers; that he bowed to the genius a thousand years hence who would accomplish what he had attempted; that he had wanted to add a poet's laurels to their family's glory but had gained ignominy instead; and, in a subsequent letter, that he had reread his work, as much of it as he had finished, and had torn it up and burned it one last time and was now "rushing toward death," for he was about to enlist in the French army and cross the English Channel in order to do battle against "the ruin threatening us all upon the seas," presumably meaning the British navy.* Fortunately the French turned him down.

*England was not threatening ruin to anyone. The facts of the matter were that Kleist (still) admired Napoleon, that Napoleon was planning an invasion of England, and that Kleist wanted to escape ignominy as a failed writer.

In the view of Kleist's biographers, these two letters to his sister mark a tragic watershed in his life; some scholars, however, dismiss especially the second one as a "rhetorical extravaganza" inflated with theatrical emotions, its "truth-content"* tending toward nil. But it is a simpleminded psychology that denies the truth of emotional rhetoric because it is not confirmed by practical action, especially when the rhetorician is a poet. Kleist did behave rationally enough in the weeks and months after he wrote the letter: he gave no signs of suicidal frenzy. Nevertheless, all the "extravagant" gestures displayed in the letters to Ulrike were eventually lived out in the plots and passions of his plays and stories—the furious ambition, the soldierly style of its pursuit, the crushing weight of an illustrious ancestry, the misery and shame of defeat, the ecstasy of self-destruction. Indeed, the drama of his life appears to be plotted along the same trajectory.

Heinrich von Kleist was the oldest son of a landless Prussian officer who counted eighteen generals among his forefathers. By this fact alone, he seemed predestined to an officer's career. He enlisted in the army when he was fifteen and in seven years rose to the rank of second lieutenant. By the time he was sixteen, both his parents had died. We may take it for granted that the Prussian army was a harsh stepparent. When he was twenty-two, he resigned his commission "in order," he wrote to his superiors, "to complete my studies." While that was true—he did enroll at the University of Frankfurt-an-der-Oder—a letter to a former teacher reveals another motive: "When the whole regiment went through its drills, it struck me as a living monument to tyranny." The performance of his function as an officer was having a bad effect on his character, so that "in addition to my natural distaste for the military profession, it was my duty to leave it." From now on, he wrote, his

*R. H. Samuel and Hilda M. Brown, *Kleist's Lost Year and the Quest for "Robert Guiskard"* (Leamington Spa, 1981), cited in Thomas Wichmann, *Heinrich von Kleist* (Stuttgart, 1988), p. 69.

ambition would be the attainment of Knowledge, Virtue, and Happiness.

In Frankfurt he proposed to a major general's daughter, Wilhelmine von Zenge, became engaged, and then, shortly before the wedding was to take place, took off on a mysterious trip to Würzburg, the purpose of which he refused to reveal to his fiancée. Nor has subsequent scholarship established a reason, having little beyond the dark hints and mystifications of Kleist's letters to guess from. The riddle of Kleist's secret mission has generated all sorts of conjectures, ranging from industrial espionage to a cure for masturbation. The theory most plausibly supported by the knowable facts suggests that, whatever the primary purpose of the trip, some kind of surgery, possibly for a phimosis, was performed on him in Würzburg, and that Kleist thought its successful outcome would make him a better husband. In any case, shortly before he left Würzburg, Kleist's letters to Wilhelmine, which ordinarily were filled with imperious moral instructions, brimmed over in blissful expectation of the joys of marriage. He was in no hurry to come home, though. Virtue demanded that he go to Berlin, there to acquire various kinds of knowledge necessary for the bureaucratic career he intended to pursue.

Several months later, a poignant letter to Wilhelmine announced the collapse of everything Kleist had believed in. He had been studying the "newest philosophy," especially Kant's idealism, and had come to a conclusion that would have horrified Kant: Since the world is unknowable through the senses, the very notion of truth constitutes a deception. The dream of knowledge had become a mirage; the lot of man now seemed inescapable uncertainty and anguish. All that was left, short of death (for which he confessed an ardent longing), was to retreat to a bucolic life in Switzerland, à la Rousseau. Wilhelmine was not inclined to follow in either of those directions, and Kleist rather coldly broke off their engagement.

Doubts have been raised about the extent and even the existence of a "Kant crisis" in Kleist's life, for the same reason that the tragic depth of his "Guiskard crisis" has been put into question. His letters, though brilliant, desperate, sad, and beautiful, are not to be trusted as sources of factual information. Kleist not only embroidered on the truth but frequently invented it, sometimes borrowing from other writers. For example, some passages of tragic confession addressed to his sister are a virtual collage of a novel by Ludwig Tieck.* An epistolary description of himself floating supine in a boat by moonlight, drifting in reverie, cradled by the lapping waves, was probably occasioned by a happy experience reading a very similar passage in Rousseau's *Rêveries*.† The "Kant crisis" letter to Wilhelmine contains similar plagiarisms and is therefore believed by some students of his life to have been written only to justify a single sentence: "Wilhelmine, let me travel."

But again, Kleist was lying for the moment and announcing a truth for the rest of his life. It may very well be that it was not his reading of Kant that unsettled him but the volcanic eruption of his own artistic vocation. There was, in any case, a crisis of faith in the ordering power of reason, and it was permanent. The "life plan" he had sought to design for himself—an absurdly airtight construction—was in ruins. "Virtue," "Happiness," and all the certitudes of Science stood like household gods at the edge of a chasm. Blind chance and absurdity took center stage, and with them an awed and brokenhearted fascination with the depth and unilluminable darkness of the human soul. His life as a poet began.

Seven years later, Johann Wolfgang von Goethe, privy councilor of the Archduchy of Weimar and Europe's most influential man of letters, received a strangely tortuous missive through the mail:

*Wichmann, pp. 32–33.
†Ibid., pp. 48–49.

Dresden

January 24, 1808

Honorable Sir!

Esteemed Privy Councilor!

*I have the honor of sending Your Excellency the
first issue, herewith enclosed, of our journal,* Phöbus. *It
is on "the knees of my heart" that I thus appear before
you; may the emotion that makes my hands uncertain
substitute for the value of what they bring.*

*I was too fearful to offer the tragedy, of which
Your Excellency will find a fragment here, to the public
in an unabridged form. As it stands here, one must perhaps admit of the premises as possible, and not take
fright later, when the corollary is drawn.*

*It is, incidentally, as little written for the stage as
that earlier drama* The Broken Jug, *and I can only
ascribe it to Your Excellency's kind and encouraging
intentions toward me if the latter should be performed
in Weimar nonetheless. The rest of our theaters are not
in a condition, on either side of the curtain, that would
give me cause to expect such an honor, and though I
ordinarily prefer to belong to the present in every
respect, I must in this case look toward the future, to
avoid looking back on results that would be too
disheartening . . .*

By now, if not earlier, the privy councilor must have
raised his eyebrows. He had already offered to perform *The
Broken Jug*, even though, in his view, it was not truly stage-
worthy. Kleist knew this. For him to send another play, un-
apologetically advertised as being imbued with the same
fault Goethe had censured in the first, had an unmistakably
contentious quality, despite the deferential tone of the letter, which could be taken to be just a touch too obeisant to
be sincere. The disparaging remarks about "the rest of our"
theaters did not appear to exempt Goethe's own. And it was
a humbled King of Judah who prayed "on the knees of my
heart" to Jehovah, hence the quotation marks around the
phrase. Could they have an ironic meaning as well?

And there was another irritating detail. The letter had come in the wake of an announcement of *Phöbus*, signed by Kleist and his coeditor, Adam Müller, that had been framed in peculiarly martial terms. Poets and writers were challenged to a race in which contestants would vie for an unattainable prize. Naturally, there could be no winners or losers in such a contest. Nevertheless, all participants would be heavily armed; unarmed or lightly armed participants would be turned away. Among the combatants would be "great authors of long-established fame." And what was Goethe to think of the magazine's cover? It was a drawing of Phoebus Apollo, the god of poetry, steering his horses above the city of Dresden, where Kleist lived, beneath an aureole consisting of six zodiacal signs, at the center and top of which stood Kleist's birth sign, Libra, flanked left and right by Goethe's and Schiller's signs, Virgo and Scorpio.*

But the greatest affront was the new play. It took up a number of themes that were dear to Goethe and turned them in a direction he could only find loathsome. Its heroine, the Amazon Penthesilea, was a devotee of Artemis, like Iphigenia, the magnanimous priestess in Goethe's most recent play. But what a difference! Iphigenia embodies a Christianized Hellas, a sublime balance of love, truth, and beauty; Kleist's warrior queen burns with despotic fury:

> *My mind's made up, you'd sooner regulate*
> *A torrent shooting down a mountainside*
> *Than rule the thundering plunge of my resolve.*

Iphigenia modestly, gently pleads the rights of womanhood, which does not share in the glory of men's deeds but knows a wisdom drawn from patience and bereavement; Penthesilea proclaims an Amazon virtue that would have terrified the guests in a Berlin drawing room, and broken their china as well:

*Katharina Mommsen, *Kleists Kampf mit Goethe* (Heidelberg, 1974), p. 74.

And would it not be madness if just now,
After five sweat-filled suns of hot pursuit
And struggling for his fall, I should relent:
Now that the breeze of a swung sword alone
Might, if it struck him, bring him down, like fruit
Grown overripe, beneath my horse's hooves?

Iphigenia is chaste; Penthesilea lusts after her mortal foe
with a carnal appetite that had never been seen in German
poetry, or by the Greeks in the play who watch the chase
from a high hill:

> *Look! With what eagerness*
> *She hugs her thighs around her charger's body!*
> *How, parched with thirst, bent low into the mane,*
> *She sucks into herself the hindering air!*

Even in joy, this woman is excessive:

> *And now, my heart, release the stagnant blood*
> *That waits, as if attending his arrival,*
> *Heaped up within both chambers of my breast.*
> *You wingèd couriers of untrammeled joy,*
> *Sweet liquors of my youth, spring forth and fly*
> *With all your might rejoicing through my veins,*
> *And let the message, like a crimson flag,*
> *Be flown through all the kingdoms of this face:*
> *The young son of the Nereid is mine!*

And who is her beloved enemy? It is Achilles, about whom
Goethe, at the time Kleist wrote his letter, was known to be
writing an epic poem. But this Achilles departs in every
respect from the alabaster virtues of neoclassical conception. He, too, is running amok, hunting his huntress,
obsessed.

Goethe's swift response was perhaps the rudest dispatch this consummately polite man sent out in a long life-
time's correspondence:

Honorable sir, I am very grateful for the copy of
Phöbus *you sent me. The prose pieces, some of which I
knew already, gave me much pleasure. As for Penthesilea, I have not yet been able to warm up to her. She is
of so wondrous a race and moves in such an alien region that I shall need time to get accustomed to both.
Also, permit me to say (for if we are not prepared to
speak out, it would be best to remain silent) that I am
always saddened and troubled when I see young men
of intelligence and talent waiting for a theater that has
yet to come. A Jew waiting for his Messiah, a Christian
for the New Jerusalem, and a Portuguese for Don Se-
bastian do not cause me greater discomfort. In front of
any makeshift platform I would say to the genuine
dramatic genius: hic Rhodos, hic salta! At every country fair, on planks over barrels, I would venture, with
the plays of Calderón, to give pleasure to the educated
and the uneducated, mutatis mutandis.* Forgive my
bluntness: it attests to my sincere good intentions. Such
things of course can be said more pleasantly and with
friendlier turns of phrase. For now, I am content to
have gotten this off my chest. More later.*

Goethe

"More later" indeed. Goethe's botched production of *The
Broken Jug* a month later casts serious doubt on the sincer-
ity of his good intentions, or else on his vaunted sagacity as
a man of the theater. The play was meant to be performed
as a single, rapid-paced movement. Goethe divided it into
three acts, with musical interludes—a bow to custom, but it
is hard to understand how a man of his experience and
ability could have failed to foresee the consequences. He
also might have introduced some judicious cuts *("mutatis
mutandis")*, as Kleist himself did eventually, or could at

---

* "with the necessary changes."

least have proposed them. This play has become one of the most popular comedies in the classical German repertory, but the effect on its first audience was bafflement, boredom, and, finally, a storm of derision. Kleist's friends had to restrain him from challenging the great man to a duel.

In the third issue of *Phöbus*, Kleist published a large portion of *The Broken Jug*, in order, he said, "to allow our readers to determine for themselves why the play failed in Weimar." After throwing down this gauntlet, he published a series of vengeful epigrams aimed at Goethe and a few that lampooned the shocked reactions of critics to what they had read of *Penthesilea*. One of these gibes announced the imminent publication of the complete play as a "canine comedy" featuring "heroes, women, and mutts." A second one, titled "Dedication of Penthesilea," burlesqued the tragedy's horrible conclusion, which, in his letter to Goethe, he had declared himself "too fearful" to reveal to the public all at once:

> *Tenderly proffered to sensitive hearts: With dogs she dismembers*
> *Him whom she loves, and then gobbles him up, hair and all.*

An enemy could not have put it more cynically; by writing it himself, he was blunting the edge of potential attacks and pronouncing himself undefeated after the debacle in Weimar.

Three years later, at the age of thirty-four, Kleist was poor and in debt, living in a room with no furniture, dependent on loans from Ulrike, who was beginning to regard him as a failure and a nuisance. He had stopped writing. In less than a decade, he had produced a life's work—eight plays, a collection of stories, essays, poems, anecdotes, and splendid letters—that would immortalize him in the eyes of a distant posterity. This decade, moreover, was by no means free of time-consuming interference and extra-literary commitments: a period of employment with the Prussian Ministry of Finance; imprisonment at the hands of occupying French troops in Prussia, who took him for a spy; a nervous breakdown; several exhausting bouts with mysterious, probably psychogenic, illnesses; voyages to France and Switzerland; the coediting of *Phöbus*, which failed largely as a consequence of the *Broken Jug* debacle; and the founding and almost single-handed editing of the *Berliner Abendblätter*, that city's first daily newspaper, to which he also contributed articles, news stories, and anecdotes. Most of these prodigious achievements had been rewarded with scant recognition and some with a good deal of abuse. His newspaper venture, for instance, had been crushed by government censorship. One of his plays, *Käthchen von Heilbronn*, had been rejected at the National Theater of Berlin in favor of the trashy comedies of the day. Another drama, *The Prince of Homburg*, was turned down by the Royal Court Theater of Prussia because its military hero fell into trances and quaked at the prospect of being hanged for insubordination. Nor had Kleist seen any of his other plays performed. Politics had long ceased to be attractive: Prussia had formed an alliance with the invader, Napoleon, against whom Kleist had longed to fight—to the death, if possible.

The idea of persuading a friend to join him in suicide—always an appealing and, one senses, strongly eroticized notion for Kleist—became his foremost preoccupation. In November 1811, he found a willing partner in Henriette Vogel, an incurably ill married woman. After making meticulous preparations and writing a series of strangely high-spirited farewell messages (a characteristic phrase in one of Kleist's suicide letters: "Her grace is dearer to me than the beds of all the empresses in the world"), the couple went to a secluded lakeside spot on the outskirts of Berlin, where Kleist shot Henriette Vogel in the heart and himself in the mouth.

3

It is women who are ultimately the cause of the total decline of our stage, and they should either not go to

the theater at all, or else special stages, separate from
men, would have to be set up for them. Their demands
for decency and morality destroy the whole nature of
the drama, and the Greek conception of theater could
never have developed if women had not been com-
pletely excluded from it.

The woman to whom Kleist addressed these unflatter-
ing words—intended to explain why *Penthesilea* could not
and probably should not be performed during his life-
time—happened to be one of the few individuals who did
not ward off the ferocity of this play by a gesture of suave
amusement or else with disgust and disdain. Perhaps Kleist
regarded his older cousin Marie as a manly exception to the
frailties of her sex, like his sister Ulrike, of whom he once
said that she had "a hero's soul in a woman's body," and
that her only feminine traits were her hips.

Ulrike von Kleist may in fact have been the prototype
for his Amazon queen, the living model whose image he
then infused with the grandeur and poetry of myth. She
was a passionate traveler, not a convenient avocation for a
woman in those days, and to give herself the practical ad-
vantages of men, she dressed like a man and was able to
pass for one easily. Apparently she liked the disguise even
when it was not needed. Kleist disapproved, and urged her
to read Rousseau, who taught that men were designed by
Nature to be active and strong, and women to please men
and exercise gentle restraint over them by the ploys of sub-
servience. Kleist's "New Year's Wish" for the year 1800 was
addressed to Ulrike:

> *Amphibian, you who inhabit two elements always,*
> *waver no longer and choose a definitive gender at last.*

Insecurity of gender appears to have been one of Kleist's secret preoccupations. He envied his sister's "masculine"
coolheadedness, since he himself was overwhelmed by
emotion at the least provocation. And for all the virility of

his style and conduct in pursuit of "immortal fame," he was, in his friendships with men, not unacquainted with sentiments proper to women as defined by Rousseau. Kleist was twenty-seven years old when he wrote the following lines to his friend Ernst von Pfuel, who later became the Prussian minister of war:

> *You restored the age of the Greeks in my heart; I could have slept with you, my dear boy; so wholly did my soul embrace you! Often, as I watched you stepping into the lake at Thun, I contemplated your beautiful body with truly maidenlike feelings. It really could have served an artist as a model. I, had I been one, could perhaps have conceived the idea of a god through it. Your small head, curly-haired, set upon a stout neck, two broad shoulders, a sinewy body, the whole of it the very picture of strength, as if modeled after the most beautiful young steer that ever bled to the honor of Zeus. Through the feeling that you awakened in me, I came to understand the whole legislation of Lycurgus, and its concept of the love of youths. Come to me! [. . .] I shall never marry, be thou my wife, my children and grandchildren!*

Note the repetition of the word "whole" and the image of wounding at the climax of the physical description—as if this dithyramb were the plea of the halved hermaphrodite for its severed self. This most combative and tough-minded of German poets (with the possible exception of Büchner), this soldier who entered the field of literature with a knight-errant's vow to tear the laurels off Goethe's head, this domineering autodidact who never tired of lecturing women about their sacred duties, could not help observing in his own mind and body, and as well in the eccentric ways of his sister, how fluid are the boundaries between those abstract blocs of identity we call masculine and feminine, and how painful is the imposition of those psychosexual dichotomies he remained committed, or compelled, to uphold. It is not surprising, therefore, to hear our seeming misogynist's creation, the Amazon Penthesilea, sounding notes like these:

> *Free as the wind upon the fallow plains*
> *Are women who have acted with such valor,*
> *And shall no longer serve the race of men.*
> *Hence let there be a sovereign nation founded,*
> *A state of women where the arrogant,*
> *Imperious voice of man shall not be heard;*
> *That gives itself its laws in dignity,*
> *Obeys itself, provides its own protection . . .*

or to hear her, moments later, deploring the fact that she was not granted "the gentler art" of seducing a man by sweet subordination:

> *On bloody battlegrounds I have to seek him,*
> *The youth my heart has chosen for its own,*
> *And this soft breast may not receive him sooner*
> *Than I have captured him with arms of bronze.*

Nor is it surprising, though the irony is extraordinary, that it was the radical women's movement of the seventies and eighties of our century—more precisely the influence of those women on the German theater—that gave this play the public acceptance and social importance that were denied it, with few and sporadic interruptions, until then. And since that same period was the heyday of the theater director's apotheosis as well—when every historic author was felt to require the tutelage of an auteur—the play, which had previously been tossed like a hot potato across the decades from one anxious, abbreviated production to the next, now became provender for a loosely scattered band of more or less willful interpreters.

The most celebrated of these was Hans Neuenfels, whose *Penthesilea* at the Schiller-Theater in Berlin in 1981 was both a multimedia extravaganza and a sociohistorical exegesis. The men were variously costumed as Prussians, Greeks, and naked savages. Achilles was a jovial, compliant, middle-aged beau. The women skipped about by candle-light in flouncy white gowns, wielding dainty bows and arrows, reminding one reviewer of the "obscene chastity" of Nazi kitsch. A hysterical Penthesilea burst from this pallid sorority like a hyena, crawled around on all fours before charging off to demolish Achilles, then came back lugging three bloody suitcases presumably filled with his remains. During the breaks, while the sets were changed, a silent film of the love-that-might-have-been was projected onto a screen, complete with a wedding feast blessed by the Amazon High Priestess.

This last device—its technique as much as its content—is symptomatic of many misreadings the play has received, both in production and in critical analysis. Like the inkblots of the Rorschach test, its seething, eruptive patterns have attracted moral, political, psychoanalytic, even religious projections that simply obliterate meanings which the play, unlike the inkblots, explicitly contains.

There is no possibility of romantic fulfillment in *Penthesilea*; there is a brief dream of love which, the audience knows, is only a desperate deception veiling, for a moment, the inescapable rules of war, including the war between the sexes. Penthesilea is obedient to these rules, as is Achilles, until the end. Her love fills the other women with incomprehension, pity, and rage, but she does not, as is frequently claimed, rebel against her nation or even break a supposed Amazon law when she sets her sights "on one head" instead of leading her armies home with their human loot. Her mother on her deathbed has given her a virtual assignment to capture Achilles, and lest there be any doubt, her friend Prothoë confirms that she has not acted in violation of custom.* And the High Priestess, far from being merely the conventional figure of traditional piety she is sometimes taken for, is the keeper of a bloody mystery, of

---

* Viz. Scene 15, p. 100.

which Penthesilea is only dimly cognizant until she discovers it in the horror of her own atrocity. That is why, in the end, she places the corpse at the High Priestess's feet. Nor is her grisly crime simply the result of pathological confusion, though the Amazons and especially the High Priestess see it that way. Penthesilea's frenzy and subsequent exhausted trance betray all the symbolic signs of possession by her nation's goddess, Artemis. The murder of Achilles is a sacrifice that consummates, before the eyes of all the Amazons, the *raison d'état* on which their nation is founded. That nation is neither a feminist heaven nor a culturally inferior, degenerate society, as some would have it, but, for all its revolutionary uniqueness, a state, and as such, just like the Greek state, and just like Kleist's Prussia or France, an embodiment of unnatural, alienated, impersonal existence, opposed to freedom and ignorant of love.*

The temptation to inject a utopian perspective into this extremely pessimistic vision is understandable, but it should be resisted. There is a utopia already present, a poetic Nowhere transcending all conflict: it is the play itself, but it must be allowed to exist as its own universe without being stuffed into alien conceptual schemata like meat into a suitcase. If someone wants to toot an ideological horn not provided for in the original score, let him do it somewhere else. I am not speaking of authority and tradition but of love and respect for the music. It need not be played on period instruments. I will cite a case in point.

In August 1990, I saw *Penthesilea* performed in Berlin by a single actress, Edith Clever, under the direction of Hans-Jürgen Syberberg. For nearly four and a half hours, she glided in and out of nine principal and a handful of subsidiary characters on the iambic waves of this crazed, violent, unearthly poem, speaking it clearly and simply, in a tone by turns wondrous, urgent, exuberant, and sorrowful, yet always as if in a trance of hypnotic removal, on a bare

* Here I am following Thomas Wichmann's astute analysis of the play, op. cit., pp. 127–40.

stage with a few arcane props (a bust of Goethe, the death masks of Kleist and Frederick the Great; candles; books; a rose; a drinking glass and a pitcher full of water), allowing the words, through her wonderfully pliant voice, to carry the entire action unassisted except by her dignified presence and a few simple gestures now and then. At one moment only, she exploded into spine-chilling histrionics. It was near the end of the play, when the Queen rouses her troops for the final battle:

> *You sickle-bladed chariots, gleaming bright,*
> *Prepare the harvest festival of war,*
> *Come, row on row, my ghastly reapers, quick!*
> *And you that thresh the crop of human corn,*
> *That it be crushed forever, seed and stalk,*
> *My mounted troops, assemble round about me!*
> *Ferocious pomp of war, unmerciful,*
> *Magnificent destroyer, on you I call!*

But imagine this ranted in the voice of Hitler, and in German, by a woman with high cheekbones and long hair parted in the middle, her fists clenched by her sides, her whole face clenched, *looking* like Hitler and at the same time like a tormented child whose rage would dearly love to tear the world to shreds. Then, in the aftermath of the disaster, the strange solemnity returns, an almost absent, musing manner, as if the whole fabulous pageant, its passionate battles and affects and tears, had been the ghostly discourse of a lost soul in conversation with itself. It was not surprising to read in the program notes that the director had wanted the performance to serve as a kind of consecration, a putting to rest of this great play's errant and homeless spirit.

JOEL AGEE

The wit who compared translations—I presume he meant translations of poems—to lovers who, if they are beautiful, are not faithful, and if they are faithful are not beautiful, had views on fidelity, translation, and beauty that I do not share. A translator's fidelity can involve a degree of self-effacement that would be frightening in a lover: complete identification with the poem and all its details, its form, voice, gestures, its secret pulse, to the point of fanaticism, to the point of pedantry: all of it must be rendered, the letter and the spirit, the whole poem. Therefore beauty, if the original is beautiful, is simply an obligation imposed by fidelity, and any imported excellence not matched by the original is instinctively felt to be an offense.

That has been my standard in translating *Penthesilea*: as faithful a concordance, on as many levels, line by line, as my ability and the character of our language would allow. Naturally, it must stand as a poem in English. And since the poem is a play, the language must also support, by qualities having more to do with the nature of physical speech than with linguistic meaning, the expressive power which actors, I hope, will give it on the stage. These, as I said, were my standards. Having said that, I am obliged to concede a measure of unavoidable compromise, and therefore of failure. The original and its reproduction are not interchangeable. But this is not altogether to be deplored. The translator's demons are the protective spirits of the poem; they remind him that each language has its own irreducible quiddity, and that poetry sinks its taproot precisely there.

German syntax, for instance, allows the disjunction of

parts of speech by intermediate constructions of labyrinthine complexity. Kleist uses this instrument to load images with emotion, phrases with propulsive energy, sentences with knotted fury, and to deploy these magnificent tangles like war machines for the liberation of affect within the stately rhythms of classical pentameter.* The aesthetic effect is both explosive and serene, and it cannot be duplicated in English. But it can be imitated, and I have striven to do so wherever it was possible without wrenching our own language out of its axis.

One critical reader suggested that I loosen up the formality of my blank verse, perhaps by taking a lesson from Wordsworth. But Kleist's catastrophic climate is not the right weather for Wordsworth's perambulations, and besides, translating Kleist is only one part of my job. The other is to translate us from our presumed vantage as "moderns," our more or less adventitious habits of thought and emotion, to Kleist and his imperishable world.

J . A .

---

* Matthieu Carrière's essay *Für eine Literatur des Krieges, Kleist* (Frankfurt a. M., 1981) brilliantly describes Kleist's martial strategies as a stylist.

NOTES ON PRONUNCIATION

I have, for the most part, adhered to English and American convention in the way I adapted the names of Kleist's characters, with a few exceptions:

PROTHOË should be pronounced as a three-syllable word: *Pro*-toh-eh. (I suggest that the "th" be pronounced as a hard "t.")

Similarly, MEROË is a three-syllable word: *Meh*-row-eh.

TANAÏS has three syllables, with the accent on the second: Ta-*nah*-is. (I suggest that the second "a" be pronounced as in "father," not as in "able.")

PENTHESILEA is a five-syllable word: *Pen*-te-sil-*lay*-uh. Here, too, I suggest avoiding the lisping "th" by pronouncing it as a "t."

DEIPHOBUS, the son of Priam, is mentioned a few times. His name will disturb the meter if it is not pronounced in three syllables: "*Day*-pho-bus."

AUTOMEDON, the name of Achilles' charioteer, is a four-syllable word with accents on the second and fourth syllable: Awe-*tah*-me-*dahn*.

THEMISCYRA, the name of the capital of the Amazon Empire, should be stressed on the third syllable: Teh-miss-*cy*-ra. (Here, too, I suggest substituting a hard "t" for the soft "th.")

J. A.

PENTHESILEA

CHARACTERS

PENTHESILEA *Queen of the Amazons*

PROTHOË

MEROË *Amazon Princesses*

ASTERIA

HIGH PRIESTESS OF DIANA

ACHILLES

ODYSSEUS

DIOMEDES *Hellenic Kings*

ANTILOCHUS

GREEKS *and* AMAZONS

Scene: A battlefield near Troy

The armies of the Greeks and Amazons
Are locked in battle like two raging wolves

SCENE ONE

[Enter ODYSSEUS *and* DIOMEDES *from one side,*
ANTILOCHUS *from the other, with soldiers.]*

ANTILOCHUS

My greetings to you, Kings! How have you fared
Since last we met before the gates of Troy?

ODYSSEUS

Badly, Antilochus. As you can see,
The armies of the Greeks and Amazons
Are locked in battle like two raging wolves.
I swear by Jupiter, they don't know why!
Unless Mars in his fury, or Apollo,
Takes them in hand, unless cloud-shaking Zeus
Cleaves them apart with storm and thunderbolt:
They will lie dead before the end of day,
Each with its teeth sunk in the other's throat.—
Bring me a helmet full of water.

ANTILOCHUS

                                   Wait!
These Amazons—what do they want of us?

ODYSSEUS

The two of us, on Agamemnon's counsel,
Set out with all the Myrmidons behind us,
Achilles and myself; Penthesilea,
We'd heard, had risen in the Scythian forests,
Leading an army, dressed in serpent skins,
Of Amazons, burning with lust for war,
By winding turns through mountainous terrain,
To shield King Priam and break our siege of Troy.
Then, by Scamander's bank, news reaches us
That Deiphobus, the Priamid, has also
Set forth in armed array, from Ilium,
To meet the Queen, who's coming near with help,

And greet her as a friend. Now we devour
The highway, hoping to forfend against
The ominous alliance of such foes
By stepping in between. All night we march.
But with the first dim reddening of dawn,
Amazement seizes us, Antilochus:
In a wide valley at our feet we see
The Amazons in combat with the troops
Of Deiphobus! And, like a hurricane
Dispersing shredded clouds, Penthesilea
Blasting the Trojan ranks in headlong sweep
As if to blow them past the Hellespont
And off the edge of Earth.

ANTILOCHUS

Strange, by our god!

ODYSSEUS

We close our ranks to shield against their flight,
Which thunders in upon us like the wedge
Of an attacking phalanx, and conjoin
Our spears to form a solid wall against them.
Beholding this, Deiphobus hesitates;
And we, conferring hastily, decide
To greet Penthesilea as an ally:
The while she, too, stems her triumphant course.
Was ever simpler, sounder counsel taken?
If I had asked Athena for advice,
Could she have whispered anything more shrewd?
She has no choice, this maiden! Having dropped
From heaven, clad for war, into our midst
To mingle in our fight—what choice has she,
Except to side with one against the other?
She must, by Hades! And we likewise must
Presume her friendly, since she battles Troy.

ANTILOCHUS

Why, yes, by the river Styx! It clearly follows.

ODYSSEUS

Well, then. Achilles goes with me to greet
The Scythian heroine where she sits mounted

In martial panoply before her maids,
Plumes flowing from her helmet, skirt tucked high,
Her palfrey tossing gold and purple tassels,
Hooves stamping on the muddy ground beneath.
For one long moment, with a pensive gaze
She stares into our ranks, void of expression,
As if we stood before her carved in stone;
This bare flat palm has more expressive features
Than were displayed upon that woman's face:
Until her glance meets that of Peleus' son:
A deepening flush spreads down unto her neck,
Blood sets her face aglow as if the world
Surrounding her were leaping into flames.
Then, with a sudden jolt, she swings herself
—Casting a somber scowl upon Achilles—
Down from her horse, and, stepping toward us, leaves
The reins with an attendant, and inquires
What brings us to her in such pageantry.
We Argives, I reply, are highly pleased
To come upon an enemy of Troy;
Long has a hatred for the sons of Priam
Consumed our hearts, I say; great benefit
Would be our joint reward if we were friends;
And other suchlike bounties of the moment.
But then I notice in the flow of talking:
She doesn't hear a word. Instead, she turns
And with a look of utter wonderment,
Suddenly like a girl, a sixteen-year-old
On her way back from the Olympic Games,
Addresses a companion by her side:
Oh Prothoë, I do not think my mother,
Otrerë, ever laid eyes on such a man!
The friend, embarrassed at these words, stays silent,
Achilles smiles at me, and I at him,
While she herself stands gazing, as if drunk
With admiration, at that glittering figure:
Until her friend reminds her timidly
That she still owes an answer to my words.

Whether from rage or shame, another blush
Staining her harness crimson to the waist,
She turns to me, confusion, wildness, pride
Commingling in her face, and speaks: I am
Penthesilea, Queen of the Amazons,
And you shall have my arrows for reply!

ANTILOCHUS
So, word for word, your messenger reported;
But no one in the entire Grecian camp
Could comprehend it.

ODYSSEUS
                              Nor could we. Not knowing
Just what to make of this display, we turn
And wend our way home, bitterly ashamed,
And see the Trojans guessing from afar
At our humiliation, and assembling
As if in triumph, with supercilious smiles,
Convinced they're the ones favored after all,
And that some error, soon to be put right,
Had drawn the Amazon's wrath upon themselves.
So they resolve to send a messenger
And offer her again the heart and hand
She'd scorned. This herald, though, has just begun
To shake the dust off his cuirass and shield,
When, sweeping in upon us one and all,
Trojans and Greeks alike, that centauress
Comes flying, reins hung slack, with all the force
And rampant frenzy of a cataract.

ANTILOCHUS
Truly astounding, Danaeans!

ODYSSEUS
                              And now begins
A struggle, friend, such as had not been fought
Since Gaia loosed the Furies on this world.
I thought till now that Nature knows but force
And counterforce, and no third power besides.
Whatever quenches fire will not bring water
Seething to a boil, nor vice versa.

8

While she herself stands gazing, as if drunk
With admiration, at that glittering figure

Yet here appears a deadly foe of each,
Upon whose coming, fire no longer knows
Whether to trickle with the floods, nor water
Whether to leap with heaven-licking flame.
A Trojan hides, hard-pressed by Amazons,
Behind a Grecian shield, the Greek defends
The Trojan from the girl, it seems as if
Argos and Troy were suddenly allied,
In spite of Helen's capture, to contend
Against the onslaught of a common foe.

[*A* GREEK *brings him water.*]

Thank you! My throat is parched.
     DIOMEDES
                            And since that day
The battle has been rumbling on this plain
Without a pause, a constant rage, as of
A storm hemmed in between steep wooded cliffs.
When I came yesterday with reinforcements
Recruited in Etolia, I arrived
Just as, with thundrous crashing, she let loose
An elemental blow, designed, it seemed,
To split all Greece down to its very roots.
The very blossom of our tribe, Ariston,
Astyanax, was shaken from the crown,
Menandros, onto that battlefield, their youth
And strength and beauty made to feed, like dung,
The laurels of that valiant bride of Mars.
More prisoners has she claimed in victory
Than she has left us eyes to mark their loss
Or arms to wrest them from captivity.
     ANTILOCHUS
And none can fathom what she wants of us?
     DIOMEDES
That's just it, no one knows, no matter where
We sink the plumb line of our thought in search.
—Often, to judge by the peculiar rage

With which, in all the tumult of the fray,
She seeks the son of Thetis, it does seem
Her heart is filled with hatred for his person.
No grim-eyed she-wolf can select her prey
And track it down, not with such hunger-heat,
Through forests decked with snow, as does this maid
Pursue Achilles through our serried ranks.
And yet there was a moment recently
When he was in her power, and with a smile
She gave him back the life he'd lost, a gift:
He'd be in Orcus now, but for her help.

    ANTILOCHUS

What? But for whose help? Hers?

    DIOMEDES

                            I tell you, hers!
For as they met in combat yesterday
At eventide, Achilles and the Queen,
Deiphobus comes, the Trojan, of a sudden,
Takes a position at the maiden's side,
And smites the son of Peleus such a savage
And cunning blow that you could hear the elms
Reverberating with the clash of steel.
The Queen turns pale, two minutes long she waits
With sinking arms: and then, indignantly,
She shakes her locks about her flaming cheeks,
And, rising tall above her horse's back,
Brings her sword plunging, like a bolt from heaven,
Down with a blaze of light into his neck,
And sends the meddler rolling to the feet
Of bold Achilles, Thetis' godlike son.
He thereupon, Achilles, wants to thank her
By dealing her a similar blow; but she,
Bent low against her piebald's flowing mane—who,
Gnashing his golden bit, throws himself round—
Eludes the murderous blow, lets the reins loose,
And turns her head, and smiles, and is gone.

    ANTILOCHUS

Most strange indeed!

ODYSSEUS
                    What news bring you from Troy?
ANTILOCHUS
I'm sent by Agamemnon, and he asks you
Whether such changed conditions don't suggest
A full retreat as our most prudent choice.
Our goal, he says, is to bring down the walls
Of Troy, not to disrupt a sovereign queen's
Campaign for stakes indifferent to our cause.
If therefore you are sure beyond a doubt
Penthesilea has not come to side with
Ilium, he wants you to return
With all your men, no matter what the cost,
Behind the Argive bastions with dispatch.
Should she pursue you, he, the son of Atreus,
Will, at the army's head, find out himself
What purpose guides this enigmatic Sphinx
Who comes to battle by the gates of Troy.
ODYSSEUS
By Jupiter! I'm of the same opinion.
Do you believe Laertes' son enjoys
Participating in this senseless fight?
Seize him, remove Achilles from the field!
For as the hunting dog unleashed flies howling
Into the antlers of the stag: the hunter,
Afraid for her, will lure and call her off;
But with her teeth locked in that glorious neck
She'll dance alongside him through mountains, streams,
And far into the woodland's night: so he,
Still raving, since the thickets of this war
Revealed to him such rare and precious game.
Retrieve him, shoot an arrow through his thighs,
And bind him tight: he swears he won't relent
Nor yield an inch to her if she retreats
Until he's seized her by her silken hair
And torn her from her spotted tiger-horse.
Why don't *you* go, Antilochus, let's see
What happens when you try your eloquence
Upon a man who's foaming at the mouth.

DIOMEDES

Kings, let us act as one, and once more, calmly,
Apply the power of reason like a wedge
To the insanity of his resolve.
Wily Odysseus, your resourceful mind
Will surely find a breach in his defense.
Should he resist, though, I and two Etolians
Shall have to carry him off upon our backs
And, since he lacks all common sense, pitch him
Just like a block of wood into our camp.

ODYSSEUS

Follow me!

ANTILOCHUS

   Wait—who's that? He's in a hurry!

DIOMEDES

Adrastus. How pale he is. He looks distraught.

SCENE TWO

[*Enter a* CAPTAIN.]

ODYSSEUS
What do you bring?
DIOMEDES
                A message?
CAPTAIN
                            Oh my lords,
The dismalest you ever heard.
DIOMEDES
                        What?
ODYSSEUS
                            Speak!
CAPTAIN
Achilles—captured by the Amazons.
And now the walls of Pergamos won't fall.
DIOMEDES
Great gods in high Olympus!
ODYSSEUS
                        Fateful news!
ANTILOCHUS
When did this horror, where did it take place?
CAPTAIN
A new attack, hot as a lightning flash,
Launched by these rage-intoxicated maids,
Melted the ranks of gallant Greeks for miles
And poured into our midst a waterfall
Of men, the undefeated Myrmidons!
We press against this frantic inundation
Of headlong flight—in vain: we're torn away,
Dragged from the field of battle, helpless, swirling:
And can't regain a foothold till the tide

Has swept us a great distance from Achilles.
And only now, spears bristling all around him,
Does he untangle himself from the night of battle,
Rolling his chariot down a fearful incline,
Racing in our direction, with our cry
Of jubilation welcoming his rescue:
Alas, the sound soon dies within our hearts,
For suddenly his horses pull up short,
Rearing before a sheer abyss, staring
Down from the clouds into a grisly depth.
Vain now his mastery of the Isthmian art,
So often and with such perfection practiced:
The team of four throw back their heads and stagger
Backward against the lashings of the whip,
And stumble in the slackened harness, falling,
A chaos of collapsing wheels and horses,
And in their midst, the son of gods, Achilles,
Supine and powerless, caught as in a snare.

    ANTILOCHUS
The maniac! How far will this——?

    CAPTAIN
                            Automedon,
His sturdy charioteer, leaps in at once
To help the sprawling horses to their feet
And raise the toppled car, but finds their thighs
Enmeshed and twisted, tangled in the traces,
And cannot free them quick enough. The Queen's
Already dashing into the ravine,
Triumphant, with a horde of Amazons,
Blocking all chances of escape.

    ANTILOCHUS
                            Great gods!

    CAPTAIN
She brings her fleeting charger to a halt,
Dust billowing around her, and lifts high
Her sparkling face to gaze up at the peak
And measure with her eye that wall of rock:
Even her helmet's crest, as if appalled,

Drags her head back and downward from behind.
Then suddenly she lays the reins aside:
We see her reeling, as if in a faint,
And pressing hastily her slender hands
Against her brow beneath its flood of locks.
Her maidens swarm around her in dismay
At this unwonted sight, imploring her,
With ardent, urgent gestures, to refrain;
The one that seems the nearest kin to her
Embraces her with tenderness; another,
More bold and willful, takes the horse's reins;
They seek by force to hinder her advance,
But she—

DIOMEDES
       What? Does she dare?

ANTILOCHUS
                 No, speak!

CAPTAIN
                     You'll hear it.
All their attempts to hold her back: in vain.
With gentle force she pushes them aside,
The women right and left, and restlessly
Trots to and fro along the rifted edge,
Seeking some narrow path that would provide
A passage for a wish that has no wings.
As if possessed, then, she begins to scale
Those jagged walls, urging her mount to leap,
Now here, now there, as if on fire with wanting,
And with the senseless hope that by this route
She'll garner her ensnared and fettered prey.
Now she has tested every ridge and fissure
Washed by the rain into the solid rock;
This precipice, she sees, cannot be scaled;
As if bereft of judgment, though, she turns
And starts her climb again from the beginning.
And actually propels herself, undaunted,
To places where no wanderer would set foot,
Swings herself closer to the topmost edge,

An elm's length nearer; and since now she's perched
Upon a rocky ledge about the width
A mountain goat would need to keep his balance,
On all sides threatened by sheer looming granite,
She dares not move a step, forward or back;
The women's shrieks of terror cleave the air:
When suddenly she tumbles, horse and rider,
Amid a clattering of loosened rocks,
A smashing fall, as if straight into Orcus,
Down to the lowest level of the cliff—
And neither breaks her neck nor learns a lesson:
She merely girds herself to climb again.
ANTILOCHUS
A raving beast she is, a mad hyena!
ODYSSEUS
Well? And Automedon?
CAPTAIN
                    He finally leaps,
For now both car and horses have been righted—
—I think Hephaestos could in all that time
Have forged a whole new chariot out of brass—
He leaps into the seat and grasps the reins:
A great unburdening relieves our hearts.
But just as he's begun to turn the horses,
The Amazons espy a hidden path
Leading in gentle incline to the peak:
They fill the valley with their jubilation,
And call their Queen, who still, as if demented,
Is trying to scramble up that precipice.
She, hearing them, throws round her charger's head,
Casts a swift glance to where the path leads upward,
And, stretched full out, just like a panther, follows
Her glance uphill at breakneck speed; Achilles,
This much I know, retreated with the horses;
But I lost sight of him among the rocks,
And what became of him, I cannot tell.
ANTILOCHUS
He's lost!

On all sides threatened by sheer looming granite,
She dares not move a step, forward or back

DIOMEDES

    Friends, we must act! What shall we do?

ODYSSEUS

The prompting of our hearts should answer that!
Kings! Let us hurry and free him from her grasp!
If that should mean a fight for life and death:
I'll be the one to face the Atrides' wrath.

[*Exit* ODYSSEUS, DIOMEDES, ANTILOCHUS.]

SCENE THREE

[The CAPTAIN *and a party of* GREEKS *who during the second scene have been climbing a hill]*

A MYRMIDON *[looking out over the countryside]*
Look! Rising up above that mountain ridge,
Is that a head I see, an armored head?
A helmet, feathers dancing up above?
The neck that bears the head, the powerful neck?
The arms, the shoulders dressed in flashing steel?
The shining breastplates, don't you see them, friends,
Down to the golden belt around his waist?
CAPTAIN
Ha! Whose!
MYRMIDON
Whose! Tell me, am I dreaming, Argives?
Now I can see the heads, adorned with blazes,
Of his four stallions! Only their haunches
And hooves are still concealed behind the ridge.
On the horizon, there it is, complete,
A chariot fit for war! Just like the sun
Rising in splendor on a clear spring day!
THE GREEKS
Hurrah! Achilles! The gods' own son! Hurrah!
Driving the four-horse chariot home himself!
He's safe!
CAPTAIN
Oh mighty gods that dwell above us,
Eternal praise be your reward! —Odysseus!
Run, someone, fetch the Argive princes, quick!

[A GREEK *goes quickly off.]*

Is he still coming closer, friends?

MYRMIDON

                Oh look!

CAPTAIN

What's that?

MYRMIDON

      Captain, it takes my breath away!

CAPTAIN

What is it, speak!

MYRMIDON

         The way, with his left hand,
He reaches far across the horses' backs!
The way he brandishes the whip above them!
The way the sound of it alone excites them!
The godly steeds! How they churn up the ground!
By Zeus, I swear the car's being drawn by vapors
That issue from their throats in trailing streams!
A hounded stag in full flight runs no faster!
The eye can't penetrate the whirling wheels,
The spokes meld into one, a solid disc!

AN ETOLIAN

Behind him, though—

CAPTAIN

                What?

MYRMIDON

                    By the mountain's edge—

ETOLIAN

Dust—

MYRMIDON

    A smoke-like dust, dark, like a storm cloud:
And, darting forth, like lightning—

ETOLIAN

                   Deathless gods!

MYRMIDON

Penthesilea.

CAPTAIN

     Who?

ETOLIAN

        The Queen herself!—

Close on the heels of Peleus' son already,
With her whole band of women following.

CAPTAIN
The raging fury!

THE GREEKS [calling]
            This way! Come to us!
Godlike Achilles, turn your course this way!
Come here, to us!

ETOLIAN
            Look! With what eagerness
She hugs her thighs around her charger's body!
How, parched with thirst, bent low into the mane,
She sucks into herself the hindering air!
She's flying as if shot straight from an iron bow!
Numidian arrows don't fly half as swiftly!
The army lags behind, like trotting curs
Left panting in a full-stretched greyhound's wake!
Her plume itself can hardly follow her!

CAPTAIN
And is she gaining?

A DOLOPIAN
            Gaining!

MYRMIDON
                        No, not yet!

DOLOPIAN
She's coming closer, Greeks! With every hoofbeat
She swallows, as if ravenous, one more piece
Of ground still separating her from him—

MYRMIDON
By all the gods protecting us on high!
She's come to loom almost as large as he is!
By now she's breathing in the wind-borne dust
Raised on the edges of his path of flight!
The horse she's riding has drawn close enough
To send the clods of earth kicked up behind him
Back into the shell of his own chariot!

ETOLIAN
And now— Oh this is reckless! This is mad!

He's turning in an arc as if to tease her.
Watch out: the Amazon will take the chord:
You see? She's intercepting him—

MYRMIDON

Help! Zeus!
She's coursing by his side now! And her shadow,
Huge, like a giant, in the morning sun,
Already slaying him!

ETOLIAN

But suddenly—

DOLOPIAN

He wrenches them abruptly, his whole team,
Off to the side!

ETOLIAN

He's flying toward us again!

MYRMIDON

Cunning Achilles! Ha! He tricked her—

DOLOPIAN

Look!
She's shooting past, thrown by her own momentum,
Into the void—

MYRMIDON

Hurtles, flies in the saddle,
And stumbles—

DOLOPIAN

Falls!

CAPTAIN

What?

MYRMIDON

Falls! The Queen, she's fallen!
And falling over her, an Amazon—

DOLOPIAN

Another one—

MYRMIDON

Again—

DOLOPIAN

And yet another—

CAPTAIN

Ha! Falling, friends?

DOLOPIAN
                    Falling—

MYRMIDON
                              Collapsing, Captain,
A molten heap, like metal in a forge,
Horses and riders thrown pell-mell together!

CAPTAIN
Would that they turned to ash!

DOLOPIAN
                              Dust all around,
And glints of arms and armor flashing through:
The eye no longer can discern a thing.
A tangled knot of maidens, interwoven
With steeds of every color: Chaos itself,
From which the world first sprang, was more distinct.

ETOLIAN
But now—a wind is rising; night turns to day;
One of them stirs and rises to her feet.

DOLOPIAN
Ha! What a busy bustling and commotion!
Look at them searching for their spears and helmets
Scattered about the field in all directions!

MYRMIDON
Three horses and an Amazon are still
Stretched out like corpses—

CAPTAIN
                              And is that the Queen?

ETOLIAN
Penthesilea?

MYRMIDON
                    Is it the Queen, you ask?
—Alas! Would that my eyes refused to serve me!
There she stands!

DOLOPIAN
                    Where?

CAPTAIN
                              Speak! Tell us!

MYRMIDON
                                        There, by Zeus!

Where she fell down; beneath that shady oak!
Supporting herself on her horse's neck,
Bareheaded—see, her helmet on the ground?—
Reaching with feeble hands into her locks
To wipe her forehead clean of dust, or blood.
            DOLOPIAN
By Zeus, it's she!
            CAPTAIN
                        She's indestructible!
            ETOLIAN
A cat, thrown down like that, would die: not she!
            CAPTAIN
And Peleus' son?
            DOLOPIAN
                        Beloved of all the gods!
Three arrow shots away he's flown, and more!
Scarcely with shaded eyes can she still reach him,
And thought itself comes to a breathless halt
Within her heart, arrested in its craving!
            MYRMIDON
Hurrah! There comes Odysseus in the distance!
The whole Greek army lit up by the sun
Comes suddenly from out the forest's night!
            CAPTAIN
Odysseus? Diomede as well? Dear gods!
—How far behind them is he in the field?
            DOLOPIAN
A stone's throw, Captain! We can see his team
Speed toward the heights along Scamander's bank,
Where rapidly the army's drawing up;
And now he thunders past their ranks—
            VOICES [*from a distance*]
                                    Hail! Hail!
            DOLOPIAN
They're calling out to him, the Argives—
            VOICES
                                    Hail!
Hail, son of Peleus! Hail, divine Achilles!
Hail to you! Hail!

He reins the horses in!
Before the Argive princes gathered there
He reins them in! Odysseus goes to meet him!
Covered with dust, he leaps from his high seat!
He gives the reins away! He turns around!
Removes the heavy helmet from his head!
And all the Kings of Argos press around him!
The Greeks, rejoicing, lift him on their shoulders,
And, swarming round his knees, carry him away;
Meanwhile, Automedon with measured step
Conducts his steaming horses by his side!
And here it comes, the swarming, jubilant
Procession! Hail to you! Godlike hero!
Oh look this way! Look here! He's here already!

SCENE FOUR

[ACHILLES, *followed by* ODYSSEUS, DIOMEDES,
ANTILOCHUS, AUTOMEDON *with the quadriga at his
side, and the* GREEK ARMY]

ODYSSEUS
My heart's most fervent welcome, hero of
Aegina! Victorious even in full flight!
By Zeus! If by your mind's supremacy
Alone, behind your back, your mortal foe
Sprawls in the dust, what will the issue be,
Divine Achilles, should you ever succeed
In seizing her directly, face to face.

[*Holding his helmet in his hand,* ACHILLES *wipes the
sweat from his brow. Two* GREEKS, *without his notic-
ing, take one of his arms, which is wounded, and ban-
dage it.*]

ANTILOCHUS
                                Son of the Nereid,
You've won a battle of contesting speeds
The like of which not even the wildest storms
Set loose to thunder across the plain of heaven
Have yet presented to the astonished world.
By the Eumenides! From my remorse
I should escape with your fleet-footed team,
Even if, grinding and creaking through the ruts of life,
My bosom's chariot-shell were loaded down
With all the weight of all the sins of Troy.

ACHILLES [*to the two* GREEKS, *whose activity appears to annoy him*]

Fools!

A GREEK PRINCE
   Who?
ACHILLES
   Why bother me —
FIRST GREEK [*bandaging his arm*]
      Hold still! You're bleeding!
ACHILLES
Well, yes.
SECOND GREEK
   Stand still, then!
FIRST GREEK
      Let us bandage you.
SECOND GREEK
It's almost done.
DIOMEDES
   Word reached us here at first
That the withdrawal of my troops had forced
You into flight; since I was occupied
In listening, with Odysseus, to the news
Antilochus was bringing us from Troy,
I was not present when this thing befell.
Yet everything I see convinces me
This masterly career of yours was taken
By choice and by design. One might well ask
Whether, when we had just begun, at dawn,
To gird ourselves for battle, you had not
Already in your mind marked out the boulder
That would bring down the Queen with such a crash:
So straightly, by the eternal gods in heaven,
So surely did you lead her to that stone.
ODYSSEUS
But now, Dolopian hero, you'll oblige,
Unless you have some better plan in mind,
By dropping back with us behind the Argive camp.
The sons of Atreus are recalling us.
We'll try to lure her, with a feigned retreat,
Into the open valley of Scamander,
Where Agamemnon lies in ambush, waiting

To bid her welcome with a grand assault.
Ah, by the god of thunder! There or nowhere
You'll cool the heat of that devouring, urgent
Fire that pursues you like a rutting buck:
And for this enterprise you have my blessing.
For to me too, she's hateful unto death,
The rampant fury, sweeping all about,
Crossing our deeds, and I'll admit I'd like it
If I could see the outline of your heel
Imprinted on her rosy-petaled cheek.

  ACHILLES [*his eye falling on the horses*]
They're sweating.

  ANTILOCHUS
     Who?

  AUTOMEDON [*feeling their necks with his hand*]
      Like melting lead.

  ACHILLES
        Good. Walk them.
And when the air has cooled them thoroughly,
Make sure to wash their chests and thighs with wine.

  AUTOMEDON
The skins are on the way.

  DIOMEDES
      Most excellent King,
We're fighting at a disadvantage here.
See for yourself: As far as sight can reach
These hills are covered with the women's hordes;
I've never seen a swarm of locusts fall
As densely squadroned on a ripe cornfield.
Who ever wins a war as he would wish it?
And is there one, beside yourself, can claim
To have so much as glimpsed the centauress?
It is to no avail that we step forward,
Dressed in gold-plated armor, and proclaim
With ringing trumpet blasts our princely rank:
She's in the background and will not come forth,
And one who even from afar would hear
Her silver voice, borne over by the wind,

Should have to fight a dubious battle first,
Devoid of honor, with a ragtag, riffraff
Legion that guards her like the hounds of hell.

ACHILLES

Is she still standing there?

DIOMEDES

You ask?—

ANTILOCHUS

The Queen?

CAPTAIN

We cannot see—away! Off with those plumes!

FIRST GREEK [*bandaging* ACHILLES' *arm*]
Wait! Just one moment.

A GREEK PRINCE

There she is, by Zeus!

DIOMEDES

Where?

GREEK PRINCE

By that oak, the one where she fell down.
Her plume is waving smartly on her head,
And her misfortune seems forgotten.—

FIRST GREEK

There!

SECOND GREEK

Now you can use your arm just as you please.

FIRST GREEK

You can go now.

[*The* GREEKS *tie a last knot and let go of his arm.*]

ODYSSEUS

Achilles, did you hear
The orders we conveyed to you?

ACHILLES

Conveyed?
No, I heard nothing. What is it you want?

ODYSSEUS

What we want? Strange— We told you what the sons

Of Atreus want! King Agamemnon's orders
Are to return posthaste to our encampment;
He sent Antilochus, if you can see him,
To bring us the supreme command's decision.
The stratagem is this: to lure the Queen
Into the vale outside the walls of Troy,
Where, caught between the two opposing armies,
And driven by the press of circumstance,
She will, perforce, declare whose friend she is;
We, thereupon, no matter what her choice is,
Shall, at the least, know what we have to do.
Your good sense, son of Peleus, will, I trust,
Obey the wisdom of this clear assignment.
For, by the Olympians, it were lunacy,
Given our urgent call to war with Troy,
If we should dally with these maidens here
Before we know just *what* they want of us,
Or *whether* they're concerned with us at all.
      A C H I L L E S [*putting the helmet back on his head*]
Go then, and fight like eunuchs, if you want;
Myself I feel a man, and to these women
I'll stand my ground, though I should stand alone!
Whether, beneath these cool pines, you continue
To skirt about her, full of powerless lust,
Far from the battle's heaving bed, or not,
Is one to me: ah, by the river Styx,
Go back to Ilium, I do not object.
What that divine maid wants of *me*, I know it;
She sends me bridal messengers enough
On feathered wing, they woo me with her wishes,
They speak with deathly whispers in my ear.
I never yet was coy with any girl;
Since first my beard began to sprout, dear friends,
I gladly yielded to them all, you know it:
If I've resisted this one to this day,
By Zeus, the god of thunder, it's because
I've not yet found the bushy trysting place
Where, undisturbed, just as her heart desires,

I'll take her in my arms on brazen pillows.
In short, go off: I'll follow in good time;
The hour of pleasure won't be long in coming:
But even if I had to court her many moons,
Or even years—I will not guide that chariot
Back to my friends, I swear this solemnly,
Nor cast eyes on the walls of Pergamos,
No, not before I've made that girl my bride
And set a crown of gashes on her forehead
And dragged her through the streets by her sleek hair.
Follow me!

    A GREEK [enters]
        Penthesilea's approaching you, Achilles!

    ACHILLES
And I her. Is she atop her Persian mount?

    GREEK
Not mounted yet. She's walking. But the Persian
Is stamping by her side already, sire.

    ACHILLES
Very good! Bring me a horse as well, my friends!
Fall in, courageous Myrmidons, and follow!

    [*The army starts off.*]

    ANTILOCHUS
He's raving mad!

    ODYSSEUS
        Your skills of rhetoric,
Antilochus, why don't you try them now!

    ANTILOCHUS
Let's hold him back by force—

    DIOMEDES
             Too late—he's gone!

    ODYSSEUS
Damnation on these women and their war!

    [*All exit.*]

SCENE FIVE

[PENTHESILEA, PROTHOË, MEROË, ASTERIA,
ATTENDANTS, *the* AMAZON ARMY]

AMAZONS
Hail to you! Hail! All-conquering! Victorious!
Queen of the Festival of Roses! Hail!
PENTHESILEA
What victory! There'll be no rose feast yet!
The battle calls me to the field once more.
That young defiant war god, I shall tame him,
Comrades-in-arms, one burning ball of light
Made from ten thousand suns were not so brilliant
As this my victory, victory over him!
PROTHOË
Beloved, I implore you—
PENTHESILEA
                                    Leave me be!
My mind's made up, you'd sooner regulate
A torrent shooting down a mountainside
Than rule the thunderous plunge of my resolve.
I want to see him sprawling at my feet,
The insolent, who on this day of battle
Like none before, worth glorious memory,
Confuses all my martial ecstasy.
Is this the conquering Queen, the fearsome one,
Who's mirrored back, as soon as I approach him,
By the steel harness covering his breast?
This, the proud empress of the Amazons?
Oh cursed by all the gods! Do I not feel,
Just when the Greeks are fleeing me all around,
That the mere sight of this one, single hero
Could touch and paralyze my inmost soul
And make me, *me*, the conquered one, the vanquished?

Where does this feeling come from that has power
To cast me down, yet has no breast to live in?
I'll throw myself into the fray of battle,
Where, with his mocking smile, he waits for me,
And overcome him, or else live no more.

PROTHOË
If you would only stay, my precious Queen,
And rest your head upon this faithful bosom.
The violence of that fall which struck your breast
Has set your blood aflame, stirred up your senses;
You're trembling, dear, in every youthful limb!
We all beseech you, make no rash decision
Until your mind regains its clarity.
Come, won't you rest with me a little while?

PENTHESILEA
How so? What happened? Why? What did I say?
Did I?— What ever did?—

PROTHOË
Just for a conquest
That tempts your young soul for a passing moment,
You would begin again the game of battles?
Because a wish, I do not know for what,
Waits unfulfilled within your secret heart,
You'd throw away, like an ill-tempered child,
The blessing that has crowned your nation's prayers?

PENTHESILEA
Ha, look at this! Accursed be this day's lot!
How they join forces with deceitful fate—
My friends, the dearest comrades of my soul—
To do me harm, to hurt me and insult me!
No sooner does my hand, desirous of
Immortal Fame as he flies past, reach out
To seize him firmly by his golden locks,
Than some power balks me with a mocking sneer—
—And I'll not yield, my soul's bent on defiance!
Begone!

PROTHOË [to herself]
Ye dwellers of Olympus, shield her!

PENTHESILEA
Am I so selfish, is it *my* desires
Alone that call me back into the field,
And not my people, not that sound I hear
Through the mad clamor of delirious triumph,
The far-off wingbeats of disaster nearing?
What have we achieved, that in the hour of Vesper
We should retire, as if our work were done?
The precious harvest, cut and bound in sheaves,
Lies heaped in high abundance in our barns,
A towering bounty, to the very heavens:
But there's a cloud of evil portent floats
Above us, pregnant with calamity.
The band of youths you captured with such valor,
You shall not guide them, to the sound of trumpets
And clashing cymbals, crowned with leaves and flowers,
Home to the fragrant valleys of your birth.
I see him lurking everywhere in ambush,
The son of Peleus, searching for the chance
To pounce upon your jubilant procession;
To follow as you guide your train of captives
Unto the battlements of Themiscyra;
Even, inside the hallowed temple walls
Of Artemis, to tear the woven chains
Of roses from their limbs, and load our own
With crushing weights and manacles of steel.
And would it not be madness if just now,
After five sweat-filled suns of hot pursuit
And struggling for his fall, I should relent:
Now that the breeze of a swung sword alone
Might, if it struck him, bring him down, like fruit
Grown overripe, beneath my horse's hooves?
No, no, unless I bring this to an end
As glorious as it was in the beginning,
Unless I firmly grasp the shimmering wreath
Above my brow, and usher Ares' daughters,
Exulting, to the very peak of fortune,
Just as I promised, let that pyramid

Come crashing down on me and them alike:
Accursed the heart that does not know restraint.

PROTHOË
My Queen, your eye burns with an alien light,
Beyond my comprehending; awful thoughts,
Dark, as if risen from eternal night,
Are turning, ominous, within my breast.
The hostile band your soul so strangely fears
Has fled before you like the winnowed chaff;
As for Achilles—you've deployed the army
So well, he's cut off by Scamander now.
Do not provoke him, just avoid his sight:
His very first step, by Jupiter, I swear it,
Will take him back to the Danaean fort.
Let *me* protect the army's rear, you'll see,
By all the Olympian gods, he won't succeed
In rescuing a single prisoner!
His glinting arms shall not alarm your troops
For miles around, nor shall the sound of hoofbeats
Disturb a maiden's laughter from afar:
For this I pledge my head as surety!

PENTHESILEA [*turning suddenly to* ASTERIA]
Can that be done, Asteria?

ASTERIA
                    Oh my Queen—

PENTHESILEA
Can I, as Prothoë demands, conduct
The troops in safety back to Themyscyra?

ASTERIA
Forgive, Your Majesty, if, for myself—

PENTHESILEA
Speak boldly. Out with it.

PROTHOË [*shyly*]
                    Would you but call
To council all your princesses and kindly
Ask them—

PENTHESILEA
                    It's *she* whose counsel I demand!

—What has become of me these last few hours?

[*Pause in which she collects herself*]

———Asteria, can I lead the army back?
Speak, can I take them safely home again?
ASTERIA
If you so wish, my Queen, let me confess,
I am astonished by the spectacle
That meets my unbelieving senses here.
You had progressed a day's march when I left
The Caucasus together with my tribe;
We could not match your army's speed, the way
You tore along just like a shooting river.
Not till this morning, as you know, at dawn
Did we arrive here, ready for the fight;
And from a thousand jubilating throats
I hear the news: the victory has been won,
Our whole campaign decided with one blow,
And all our purposes already met.
Glad, I assure you, that the people's prayer,
Without my help, has been so quickly granted,
I give out orders to prepare my troops
And horses to return. Curiosity,
Though, prods me to examine what we've won,
The band of youths whose praises I've been hearing.
And there I find a sad handful of slaves,
Pale, shivering, the Argives' very dregs,
Picked up like gleanings by your baggage train
And carried off on shields they'd thrown away.
Outside the lofty walls of Troy there stands
The whole Hellenic army: Agamemnon,
And Menelaos, and Ajax, Palamede;
Odysseus, Diomede, Antilochus;
They still defy you and are not afraid:
Yes, and the Nereid's young son, Achilles,
Whom your hand ought to decorate with roses,
He's still outbraving you, the insolent;

35

He'll plant his foot, he says—and he proclaims it
In all directions—on your queenly neck:
And Ares' peerless daughter asks of me
If she may lead the armies home in triumph?

    PROTHOË [*passionately*]

The Queen, you hypocrite, brought to their knees
More noble, brave, and handsome—

    PENTHESILEA

                        Silence, wretch!
Asteria feels as I do, there's but one
Worth bringing to his knees: and that one still
Stands confident upon the battlefield and mocks me!

    PROTHOË

Your Majesty, surely you'll not let passion
Be your—

    PENTHESILEA

          Viper! Arrest and bind your tongue!
—Unless you want to dare your Queen's wrath! Go!
Out of my sight!

    PROTHOË

              Then my Queen's wrath I'll dare!
I'd rather not behold your countenance
Again than be this moment's coward and stand,
A flatterer and traitor, by your side.
You are on fire, consumed from head to toe,
And hence not fit to lead the maidens' war:
Yes, no more fit than is a lion to match
Himself against a spear, once he has drunk
The poison cunningly set out for him.
In this condition, by the eternal gods,
You will not win the son of Peleus, ever:
Instead, before the day is done, I promise,
The youths we took in battle and hold captive,
The prize of such incalculable pains
And peril, will, by your lunacy, be lost.

    PENTHESILEA

Why, this is most peculiar, quite confounding!
What makes you suddenly afraid?

PROTHOË

Afraid?

PENTHESILEA

Who is your prisoner? Pray tell.

PROTHOË

Lykaon,
The young Arcadian prince, his army's leader.
I think you saw him yesterday.

PENTHESILEA

Yes, yes,
I do believe I saw his drooping plume
Where he stood trembling near the others—

PROTHOË

Trembling!
He stood as firm as ever Peleus' son
Stood up to you! My arrows brought him down,
And it was at my feet he sank, and proud
As any I shall lead him, at the Feast
Of Roses, to the holy temple's shrine.

PENTHESILEA

Ah, is that so? My, my, how enthusiastic.—
Very well—he won't be torn away from you!
Attendants, fetch him from the band of captives!
Lykaon, the Arcadian, bring him here!
—Take him, unwarlike maiden, take him with you,
Flee with him, lest you lose him, far away
From all the noise of battle, hide yourselves
Beneath soft stacks of sweetly fragrant elder,
In the most far-off mountain caves, where you
Can hear the nightingale's voluptuous call,
And celebrate it now, lascivious girl,
The feast your soul cannot await with patience.
But be forever banished from my sight,
And from the capital, and let your comfort
And consolation be your lover's kisses,
When everything, fame, motherland, and love,
And Queen, and bosom friend, are lost to you.
Go now, relieve me—go! I will hear nothing!

37

Remove your hateful presence from my sight!

MEROË

Oh Queen!

ANOTHER PRINCESS [*among her retinue*]
Such frightful words—

PENTHESILEA
Silence, I say!
Whoever pleads for her will meet with vengeance!

AN AMAZON [*enters*]
Achilles is approaching you, my Queen!

PENTHESILEA
Approaching— Maidens, rouse yourselves to battle!
Give me the most straight-striking spear, oh bring
Of all our flashing swords the lightning-sharpest!
Good gods, this pleasure you must grant me yet,
To throw that youth, so hotly coveted,
Tumbling into the dust before my feet.
For this I'll gladly forfeit the full measure
Of happiness allotted to my life.—
Asteria! You will lead out the troops.
Keep the Greek host engaged and see to it
That nothing thwart my ardor in the fight.
Not one of you, no matter who she be,
May strike Achilles down. A shaft of death
Is sharpened for the one who dares lay hand
Upon his head—what am I saying, upon
A single lock of his! I, only I
Know how to fell him. Comrades, this metal here
Shall draw him with the tenderest embrace
(Since it's with metal that I must embrace him!)
Closely, and painlessly, unto my heart.
You flowers of spring, lift yourselves toward his fall,
That he not injure any of his limbs.
I'd sooner lose my own heart's blood than his.
I will not sleep nor rest till from the airs,
Like some rare, bright-hued bird, I've made him plummet
Down to my feet; but once he lies before me,
Prostrate, with splayed, disabled wings, oh maidens,

To throw that youth, so hotly coveted,
Tumbling into the dust before my feet

And not a mote of crimson dust displaced,
Then, only then, may all the blessed souls
Descend to join us in our victory rites,
Homeward we'll turn our jubilant procession,
Then I'll be Queen of the Feast of Roses for you!—
Now come!—

> [*As she is about to exit, she sees the weeping* PROTHOË *and turns, distressed. Then suddenly, falling upon her neck*—]

                    Prothoë! Sister of my soul!
Will you go with me?
          PROTHOË [*in a broken voice*]
                         To the depths of Orcus!
And could I meet the Blessed without you?
          PENTHESILEA
You, better than all humankind! You'll do it?
Come, then, we'll fight and conquer side by side,
The *two* of us or *neither*, and our motto:
Roses to decorate our heroes' temples,
Or else two cypresses to crown our own.

> [*All exit.*]

SCENE SIX

[*Enter the* HIGH PRIESTESS *of Diana with her* PRIEST-
ESSES. *They are followed by a group of* YOUNG GIRLS
bearing baskets of roses on their heads, and by the PRISON-
ERS, *led by several armed* AMAZONS.]

HIGH PRIESTESS
Now, my beloved little rose maidens,
Let me behold the fruit of your excursion.
Here, by this solitary foaming spring,
Beneath the pine tree's shade, we shall be safe:
Come pour your harvest out before me here.
A YOUNG GIRL [*pouring out her basket*]
Look at the roses I picked, holy Mother!
ANOTHER GIRL [*likewise*]
This lapful here is mine!
A THIRD GIRL
                    And this one's mine!
A FOURTH GIRL
And here's a whole lush springtime just from me!

[*The other* YOUNG GIRLS *follow suit.*]

HIGH PRIESTESS
It blooms just like the peak of Mount Hymettus!
Now such a day of blessing, oh Diana!
Has never risen yet upon your tribes.
The mothers bring me, and the daughters, gifts;
And I'm so dazzled by this double splendor,
I know not who deserves the greater thanks.—
But is this your entire provision, children?
FIRST GIRL
More than you see here wasn't to be found.
HIGH PRIESTESS
It seems your mothers were more diligent.
SECOND GIRL
It's easier to gather prisoners

Upon these fields than roses, holy Priestess.
While closely pressed, on all the hills around,
The crop of young Greeks stands as if awaiting
A nimble harvester to mow them down,
So sparsely blooms in all the vales the rose,
And so well fortified, I can assure you,
That one would rather slash her way through arrows
And spears than brave their tanglework of thorns.
—Just look at these my fingers, if you will.

THIRD GIRL

I dared to step out on a jutting rock,
Only to pluck a single rose for you.
Just faintly through its dark green calyx leaves
It shimmered out at me, a little bud,
Not open yet to the full bloom of love.
I plucked it, though, and tripped, and of a sudden
Fell into an abyss, so deep, I thought
I'd sunk into the night-dark womb of death.
But it was my good luck, for such a blaze
Of roses stood there, we could celebrate
Ten Amazonian victories if we wished.

FOURTH GIRL

I plucked a rose for you, our holy Priestess,
A single, solitary rose, just one;
But what a rose it is—here, this one, see:
Fit to adorn the garland of a king.
Penthesilea herself will want none finer
After she fells the son of gods, Achilles.

HIGH PRIESTESS

So be it; when Penthesilea has felled him,
You shall present her with this royal rose.
Just take good care of it till she returns.

FIRST GIRL

From now on, when the Amazonian army
Sets out for war again with cymbals clashing,
We shall ride with them, but please promise this,
Not just to gather roses and wind wreaths
To glorify our mothers' victories.
This arm, see, can already throw a javelin,

And my sling whirls its missile to the mark:
You'll see, my own wreath blooms for me already.
—For all I know, he may right now be fighting
Bravely, the youth for whom this bow's drawn taut.

HIGH PRIESTESS

Really? —Well, I imagine you must know.
—And have you viewed the flowers with him in mind?
—When spring comes round again, they'll be in bloom
And you'll be searching for him in the fray.
—But now your mothers' glad hearts urge us on:
Wind all these roses into garlands, fast!

GIRLS [all together]

Let's get to work! How do we go about it?

FIRST GIRL [to the SECOND]

Come here, Glaucothoë!

THIRD GIRL [to the FOURTH]

Come, Charmion!

[They sit down in pairs.]

FIRST GIRL

This garland here's being woven for Ornythia,
Who won Alcestis of the towering crest.

THIRD GIRL

Ours, sisters, is Parthenion's: she'll bind
Bold Athenaeus of the Gorgon shield.

HIGH PRIESTESS [to the armed AMAZONS]

Well, don't you want to entertain your guests?
—Don't stand about so awkwardly, my maidens,
As if I had to teach the ways of love!—
Will you not venture them a friendly word?
Not hear what they, exhausted from the battle,
Might wish or want of you? Or what they need?

FIRST AMAZON

They say they don't want anything at all.

SECOND AMAZON

They're mad at us.

THIRD AMAZON

The moment one comes near them

The crop of young Greeks stands as if awaiting
A nimble harvester to mow them down

They turn away with looks of scorn and spite.

HIGH PRIESTESS

Why, if they're angry with you, then, by our goddess,
Make them amenable! Why did you have to
Strike them so fiercely in the battle's rage?
Tell them what lies in store: that will console them,
And they'll no longer be so hard to please.

FIRST AMAZON [*to a captured* GREEK]

Would you not rest your limbs, oh noble youth,
On a soft carpet? Shall I make a couch
Of vernal flowers for you, who look so tired,
Beneath the shadow of that laurel tree?

SECOND AMAZON [*likewise*]

Shall I mix the most fragrant Persian oil
In water fresh drawn from this mountain spring
To bathe and to refresh your dusty feet?

THIRD AMAZON

Surely you won't refuse the juice of oranges
Brought to you lovingly with my own hand?

ALL THREE AMAZONS

Speak! Say something! What can we do to serve you?

A GREEK

Nothing!

FIRST AMAZON

　　　　Peculiar foreigners, what ails you?
Now that our arrows rest inside their quivers,
Why do you flinch from looking at us still?
Is it our lion skins that frighten you?—
You, with the belt, speak! What are you afraid of?

THE GREEK [*after giving her a sharp look*]

Those garlands, who are they being wound for? Tell us!

FIRST AMAZON

Who? You! Who else?

THE GREEK

　　　　　　　For us! And to our face
You tell us, monsters! Do you plan to lead us
Like beasts, bedecked with flowers, to sacrifice?

FIRST AMAZON

To the shrine of Artemis! What do you think?

To her dark oaken grove, where ecstasy
Beyond constraint or measure shall be yours!

THE GREEK [*astonished, in a low voice, to the other
prisoners*]

Was ever a dream so strange as here the truth?

SCENE SEVEN

[*Enter an* AMAZON CAPTAIN.]

CAPTAIN
To come upon you here, my reverend Mother!
—A stone's throw from this place, we've mobilized
The troops for one last bloody confrontation!
HIGH PRIESTESS
The troops! Impossible! Where?
CAPTAIN
                                        In the gorges
Scamander has licked out. If you'll but listen
Into the wind that's blowing from the mountains,
You'll hear the Queen's voice thundering out commands,
The metal ring of weapons drawn, and neighing,
And blasting trumpets, bugles, cymbals, clarions,
The very voice of brazen war itself.
A PRIESTESS
Who will fly quickly up that hill?
GIRLS
                                        Me! Me!

[*They climb the hill.*]

HIGH PRIESTESS
The Queen!—No, speak! It's not to be believed—
—Why, if the battle hasn't spent its rage,
Would she give orders for the Feast of Roses?
CAPTAIN
She ordered what? The rose feast? But to whom?
HIGH PRIESTESS
To me! To me!
CAPTAIN
            Where? When?

HIGH PRIESTESS

Moments ago,
Under that obelisk in the shade I stood,
When Peleus' son, and she hard on his heels,
Swept past me swifter than the winds themselves.
And I called after her: "What news? How goes it?"
"On to the Feast of Roses, as you see!"
That's what she said; then, from afar, she cried:
"And let's not lack for blossoms, holy Mother!"

FIRST PRIESTESS

Do you see her? Speak!

FIRST GIRL [*on the hill*]

We don't see anything!
We can't make out a single plume down there,
Only the shadow of a thundercloud
Racing across the wide plain, and the surge
Of scattered groups of warriors pressing on,
Seeking each other on the fields of death.

SECOND PRIESTESS

No doubt she intends to cover our retreat.

FIRST PRIESTESS

I think so too.—

CAPTAIN

I'm telling you, she's girt
For bloody battle with the Peleid,
Fresh as the Persian horse that rears beneath her,
Pawing the air; she's facing him right now,
More fire in that flashing eye than ever,
Her breath deep-drawn, exultant, free,
As if her warrior's bosom were just now
Receiving the first heady air of battle.

HIGH PRIESTESS

What, by the Olympians, is she trying to do?
When all the woods around us are aswarm
With captives taken by the tens of thousands,
What could be left and worth her conquering?

CAPTAIN

What could be left and worth her conquering?

GIRLS [*on the hill*]
Oh gods!

FIRST PRIESTESS
What is it? Is the shadow gone?

FIRST GIRL
You holy ones above, come here!

HIGH PRIESTESS
Speak out!

CAPTAIN
You ask what's left and worth her conquering?

FIRST GIRL
Look! Look! See how the sun shines through a tear
In that black cloud, throwing a mass of light
Onto the helmet of the Peleid!

HIGH PRIESTESS
Whose helmet?

FIRST GIRL
His, I said! Whose would it be?
High on a hilltop glittering he stands,
Encased in steel his horse and he, the sapphire,
The chrysolite don't shed such brilliant rays!
The earth around, in all its bloom and color,
Cloaked in the blackness of a stormy night;
It serves but as a ground, a dusky foil
To set off this lone jewel's magnificence!

HIGH PRIESTESS
Of what concern's the Peleid to our people?
Does it behoove a child of Mars, a queen,
To take her stand upon a single name?

[*To an* AMAZON]

Make haste, Arsinoë, and step before her,
And tell her in the name of Artemis
That Mars himself has come before his brides:
That by the wrath of Artemis I charge her
To crown the god with garlands, bring him home,
And in her temple start without delay

The Festival of Roses in his honor!

[*Exit the* A M A Z O N.]

Who ever heard of anything so mad!
FIRST PRIESTESS
Girls! Have you not caught sight of her by now?
FIRST GIRL [*on the hill*]
Yes! The whole field is shining—there she is!
SECOND PRIESTESS
Where do you see her?
FIRST GIRL
                    In front of all the maidens!
All sparkling in her golden panoply,
Look at her dancing toward him for the fight!
It's just as if, spurred on by jealousy,
She wanted to speed past the very sun
That kisses his young brow! Oh look at her!
If she were trying to vault right up to heaven
And prove herself her lofty rival's peer,
Her warhorse, eager to carry out her wish,
Would tread the air with just this wingèd lightness!
HIGH PRIESTESS [*to the* CAPTAIN]
Was there not even one among the maidens
Who gave her warning or who held her back?
CAPTAIN
Her whole suite threw themselves into her path,
And all her princesses; and Prothoë
Did everything within her power, right here!
Exhausting all the arts of eloquence
To move her to return to Themiscyra.
But she seemed not to hear the voice of reason:
Of Cupid's arrows the most poisonous,
It is believed, has struck her youthful heart.
HIGH PRIESTESS
What are you saying?
FIRST GIRL [*on the hill*]
                    Ha, they're meeting now!

Dear gods, please hold your Earth and keep it firm—
Now, at this moment, as I speak, they're flying
Into each other, crashing, like two stars!

HIGH PRIESTESS [*to the* CAPTAIN]

The Queen, you say? Impossible, my friend!
By Cupid's arrow stricken— When? And where?
She who inherited the diamond belt?
Mars' daughter, she who lacks the very breast
At which those poison-feathered darts are aimed?

CAPTAIN

At least that's how the people's voice would have it,
And Meroë just confided it to me.

HIGH PRIESTESS

Oh horror!

[*The* AMAZON *returns.*]

CAPTAIN
             Well? What do you bring? Speak out!

HIGH PRIESTESS

My message, did you give it to the Queen?

AMAZON

It was too late, Your Holiness, forgive.
I glimpsed her here and there, but was unable
To find her in the whirl of women around her.
However, for a moment I did meet
With Prothoë, and told her of your will;
But she replied with words— Your Holiness,
I may have heard her wrongly in that din.

HIGH PRIESTESS

What were the words?

AMAZON
                    She halted on her horse,
And turned, with tearful eyes, it seemed, to gaze
Upon the Queen. And after I had told her
How very incensed you were that in her madness
She would prolong the war for a single head,
She said to me: Go back to her who sent you,

And bid her kneel upon the ground and pray
That this one head fall to her in the fight;
If not, there is no hope for her or us.

HIGH PRIESTESS

How steep, how straight the downward path she's taken!
And when she falls, the enemy that fells her
Will be the one she meets within her breast.
She's tearing us all with her even now;
I see the keel that bears us, bound, to Hellas,
Bright with the mockery of its festive flags,
Already foaming through the Hellespont.

FIRST PRIESTESS

Here comes the news of our undoing already.

SCENE EIGHT

[*Enter an* AMAZON COLONEL.]

COLONEL
Flee, Priestess! Save the captives while you can!
The whole Greek army's flying in our direction.
HIGH PRIESTESS
Ye gods of high Olympus! What has happened?
FIRST PRIESTESS
Where is the Queen?
COLONEL
                        She's fallen in the fight,
And the whole Amazonian army's scattered.
HIGH PRIESTESS
What are you saying! Have you lost your senses?
FIRST PRIESTESS [*to the armed* AMAZONS]
Remove the prisoners!

[*The* PRISONERS *are led away.*]

HIGH PRIESTESS
                        Now speak: Where? When?
COLONEL
Hear my report: I'll tell the worst very briefly!
Achilles and the Queen, with lances poised,
Meet on the field with a resounding crash,
Two thunderbolts colliding in mid-heaven;
Their lances, weaker than their breasts, are split;
He, Peleus' son, still stands; Penthesilea
Sinks down, unhorsed, death's shadow close upon her.
And now that she's laid bare to his revenge,
Sprawled in the dust before him, who could doubt
He'll send her flying all the way to Orcus;

But pale he stands, incomprehensible,
Himself a shade of death. Oh gods! he cries,
How she did move me with that dying look.
He quickly swings himself out of the saddle;
And while the maidens, overcome by terror,
Stand as if riveted, remembering
The Queen's command, and dare not raise a sword,
He brashly nears where she lies deathly pale,
Bends over her, Penthesilea! he cries,
Lifts her up in his arms, and carries her,
And calling curses down on his own deed,
Moaning with grief, he woos her back to life!

HIGH PRIESTESS
What? He himself?

COLONEL
                    The entire army thunders
"Fiend! Let her go!"; and "Death be his reward,"
Shouts Prothoë, "unless he leaves this place:
Give him no quarter, shoot your straightest shafts!"
And, with her horse's kicks, she drives him back
And deftly tears the Queen from his embrace.
She, meanwhile, has awoken, pitiful,
A rattling in her throat, her breast torn,
Her hair disheveled, and is led away
Behind the army's lines, where she recovers;
But this incomprehensible Dolopian—
Inside that carapace of brass, a god
Has melted down his heart with flames of love—
He's calling out to us: "Wait, friends, don't go!
Achilles greets you with eternal peace!"
And throws away his sword, throws down his shield,
And, tearing all the armor from his breast—
We could destroy him easily, with clubs,
With our bare hands, were we allowed to touch him—
He follows after her with fearless step:
The mad audacity! As if he knew
His life has become sacred to our arrows.

HIGH PRIESTESS
Who issued this insane command?

And, tearing all the armor from his breast,
He follows after her with fearless step

COLONEL

                        The Queen!
Who else?

HIGH PRIESTESS

            Oh this is horrible!

FIRST PRIESTESS

                    Look, look!
There, led by Prothoë, limping, tottering,
A sight to make one weep, the Queen, she's here!

SECOND PRIESTESS

Eternal gods in heaven! What a sight!

SCENE NINE

[*Enter* PENTHESILEA, *led by* PROTHOË *and* MEROË,
with retinue.]

PENTHESILEA [*in a feeble voice*]
Set all the dogs on him! The elephants,
Lash them with firebrands so they'll trample him!
Strap sickles on the cars and mow him down,
Slice off those rank, luxuriant limbs of his!
PROTHOË
My love! We all implore you—
MEROË
                                    Listen, please!
PROTHOË
He's close upon your heels, the Peleid;
If your life's dear to you at all, then flee!
PENTHESILEA
This bosom, Prothoë, how could he strike it
So shattering a blow? —As if I were
To smash a lyre because the night wind stirred it
My name to whisper softly to itself.
I'd nestle in between the great bear's paws,
And stroke the panther's fur, that came to me
With such emotion as I brought to him.
MEROË
You won't escape, then?
PROTHOË
                                    You refuse to flee?
MEROË
Refuse to save yourself?
PROTHOË
                                    And the unnameable,
Is this the place where it will come to pass?
PENTHESILEA
Is it my fault that on the battlefield

I have to court his feeling with a sword?
When I assault him, what is it I want?
Is it to throw him headlong into Orcus?
All that I want, eternal gods in heaven,
Is but to draw him down upon this breast!

PROTHOË
She's mad—

HIGH PRIESTESS
    Poor stricken soul!

PROTHOË
         She's lost her senses!

HIGH PRIESTESS
She has no thought except of that one man.

PROTHOË
That fall, I fear, has utterly deranged her.

PENTHESILEA [with forced composure]
Good. As you wish. So be it. I'll be calm.
This heart—since it must be, I'll subjugate it,
And with good grace submit to bitter need.
And you are right. Why should I, like a child,
Because a fleeting wish was never granted,
Break with my gods? Come, let us leave together.
I won't deny I wanted happiness.
But if it does not drop to me from heaven,
I will not storm the clouds to bring it down.
Help me to leave this place, bring me a horse,
And I will lead you back to Themiscyra.

PROTHOË
Blessed, Your Majesty, oh three times blessed be
A word so worthy of a queen as this.
Come, all is ready for our flight—

PENTHESILEA [noticing the wreaths of roses in the
children's hands, suddenly flaring up]
        Ha, look!
Who ordered you to gather all these roses?

FIRST GIRL
How can you ask that, or have you forgotten?
Who else but—

PENTHESILEA
                              Who?
HIGH PRIESTESS
                              We were to celebrate
Your maidens' long-awaited victory rites.
Was it not your own lips that ordered this?
PENTHESILEA
A curse upon this vile, impatient haste!
A curse upon the thought of sacred orgies
While blood still foams around the murderous fray!
A curse upon desires that, in the breast
Of Mars' chaste daughters, bay like an unleashed pack
Of hounds, drowning the brazen lungs of trumpets
And silencing their officers' commands!
Is victory mine yet, that with hellish scorn
My triumph should be drawing near already?
—Out of my sight!

[*She slashes the wreaths to pieces.*]

FIRST GIRL
                              Your Highness! What are you doing?
SECOND GIRL [*picking up the roses*]
The spring, for miles around, has nothing more
To give you for the feast—
PENTHESILEA
                              The spring—would that it
Withered! Would that the star on which we breathe
Lay broken on the ground like one of these!
Would that the whole celestial wreath of worlds
Could be dismembered like some woven flowers!
—Oh Aphrodite!
HIGH PRIESTESS
                    Poor unhappy thing!
FIRST PRIESTESS
Merciful gods, she's lost!
SECOND PRIESTESS
                              I think her soul

Has fallen prey to the Eumenides!

A PRIESTESS [*on the hill*]

The Peleid, oh maidens, I implore you,
He's but an arrow's flight away from us!

PROTHOË

I beg you on my knees, then—save yourself!

PENTHESILEA

Oh dear—my soul is weary unto death!

[*She sits down.*]

PROTHOË

You terrify me! What—?

PENTHESILEA

Flee if you will.

PROTHOË

You're not—?

MEROË

You won't—?

PROTHOË

You're not—?

PENTHESILEA

I'm staying here.

PROTHOË

What, are you mad!

PENTHESILEA

You hear me. Leave me be.
I cannot stand. Am I to break my bones?

PROTHOË

Most wretched of all women! And Achilles,
He's coming, do you hear, one arrow's—

PENTHESILEA

Let him.
I don't care, let him plant his steel-shod foot
Upon this neck. Why, tell me, should two cheeks
That bloom like these be any different from
The mire of which they're born? So let him come
And drag me headlong home behind his horses,

And let this body, full of warmth and life,
Be thrown upon the open field in shame.
Let me be served as breakfast for his dogs,
As offal for the hideous birds. Let me be
Dust instead of woman without charm.

PROTHOË

Oh Queen!

PENTHESILEA [*tearing off her necklace*]
            Away with these damned trinkets. Off!

PROTHOË

Eternal gods above! Is this the calm
Your own lips promised just a moment past?

PENTHESILEA

And you there, nodding on my head—be damned,
More helpless even than arrows or a face!
—I curse the hand that for the fight today
Adorned me, and the deceiving tongue that said
It was for victory, I curse them all.
How they stood round with mirrors right and left,
The hypocrites, praising my slender limbs'
Divine proportions cast in shining bronze.—
A thousand plagues upon your hellish arts!

GREEKS [*offstage*]

Onward, oh Peleid! And don't lose heart!
Move on! A few more steps and you shall have her!

PRIESTESS [*on the hill*]

Diana! Queen! If you don't leave right now,
You're lost!

PROTHOË
            Sister! My dearest heart! My life!
So you won't flee? Won't leave?

[PENTHESILEA *bursts into tears and leans against a
tree.*]

PROTHOË [*suddenly moved, sitting down beside her*]
                    Do as you will.
If you cannot, will not—so be it! Please don't cry.

I'll stay with you. What cannot be, *is* not;
What lies outside the precinct of your power,
What you *cannot* achieve: the gods forbid
That I demand it of you! Maidens, go,
Go home to your ancestral meadowlands:
The Queen and I, we're staying here together.

HIGH PRIESTESS

What, wretched girl, you would encourage her!

MEROË

Not in her power to flee?

HIGH PRIESTESS

       Not in her power,
Since nothing holds her from outside, no fate,
Only her foolish heart—

PROTHOË

       That *is* her fate!
To you, steel fetters seem unbreakable,
Is it not so? Yet she might break them, see,
But not this feeling you hold up to scorn.
What force compels her, only she can know,
And every breast that feels is an enigma.
She strove to reach the highest prize of life,
She touched it, grasped it; now her hand refuses
To stretch out to another, lesser thing.—
Come, let it be fulfilled upon my breast.
—What is it? Why the tears?

PENTHESILEA

       Pain, pain—

PROTHOË

Where?

PENTHESILEA

 Here.

PROTHOË

    What can I—?

PENTHESILEA

       Nothing, nothing, nothing.

PROTHOË

Now calm yourself; soon it will all be over.

HIGH PRIESTESS [*in a subdued voice*]
I dare say you're both mad—!
PROTHOË [*likewise*]
                    Be still, I beg you.
PENTHESILEA
If I were yet to flee—if I should do it:
How would I calm myself?
PROTHOË
                    You'd go to Pharsos.
There you would find, for that is where I sent them,
Your scattered troops completely reassembled.
You would find rest, and you would tend your wounds,
And with the morning ray, if so you pleased,
You would take up again the maidens' war.
PENTHESILEA
If I were capable—! *If* I could do it—!
The utmost human powers can achieve,
I have achieved—tried the impossible—
Staked all on one throw—everything I have;
Now the deciding die is cast, is cast:
And I must comprehend it—that I've lost.
PROTHOË
No, no, my dearest heart, do not believe that.
You must not estimate your strength so lowly.
You cannot think so poorly of that prize
For which you gamble, that you should believe
Its worth had been expended in the effort.
Was that pearl necklace, white and red, that rolled
About your throat, your whole prosperity,
The only wealth on which your soul might draw?
How much you haven't thought of yet could still
In Pharsos be accomplished for your cause!
Though now, it's true—it almost is too late.
PENTHESILEA [*after an uneasy gesture*]
If I moved quickly——ah, this drives me mad!
—Where stands the sun?
PROTHOË
                    There, right above your head;

Before night falls you'd be arriving there.
The Greeks would never know: We could join forces
With the Dardanians, quietly advance
Up to the sea cove where they lie at anchor;
At night, upon a signal, they go up
In flames, we rush their camp and overrun it,
The army, pressed from the front and from the rear,
Is torn, dismembered, scattered far and wide,
Chased, tracked down, captured, and with roses crowned
Is every handsome head we may desire.
Oh bliss if I were yet to see it happen!
I would not rest, beside you I would fight,
Not shun the heat of day, nor would I tire,
And though my limbs should shrivel from the effort,
Till my beloved sister's wish was granted,
And conquered, finally, after such toils,
The son of Peleus sinks down at her feet.

> PENTHESILEA [*who during* PROTHOË*'s speech has
> been gazing fixedly at the sun*]

Would that with widespread, rushing wings I could
Cut through the air—!

> PROTHOË

               What?

> MEROË

                       What did she—?

> PROTHOË

                                 My Queen,

What do you see?

> MEROË

               What are you looking at?

> PROTHOË

Beloved, speak!

> PENTHESILEA

               Too high, I know, too high—
In flaming rings, eternally removed,
He circles playfully around my aching heart.

> PROTHOË

Who does that, my beloved Queen?

PENTHESILEA

                              Very well.
—Where is the way?

[*She collects herself and stands.*]

MEROË

              You are deciding, then?
PROTHOË

You're rising to your feet?—Then, oh my Princess,
Let it be like a giant! If the whole weight
Of hell bears down upon you, do not falter!
Stand, stand as does the vaulted arch stand firm
Because each of its blocks inclines to fall!
Present your head, the keystone, to the gods
And all their gathered lightning, and cry: Strike!
And let yourself be split from head to toe,
But do not waver in yourself again
So long as one breath still has power to bind
The stones and mortar in this youthful breast.
Come. Take my hand.

PENTHESILEA

                    Is this the way, or that?
PROTHOË

The cliff is the less dangerous way to go,
Or you could take the easier path, the valley.—
Which way will you decide?

PENTHESILEA

                        I'll take the cliff!
That way I'll reach him sooner. Follow me.

PROTHOË

Reach whom, my Queen?

PENTHESILEA

                  Lend me your arm, dear friends.

PROTHOË

As soon as you have climbed that hillock there
You will be safe.

MEROË

              Let's go then, come.

PENTHESILEA [*suddenly stopping midway across a bridge*]

But listen:
There still remains one thing for me to do.

PROTHOË

Remains?

MEROË

What would that be?

PROTHOË

Unhappy soul!

PENTHESILEA

One more thing, friends, and I would be insane,
You must admit, if I did not explore
The field of possibility completely.

PROTHOË [*with irritation*]

Then would that we were swallowed up already!
For now there is no hope.

PENTHESILEA [*startled*]

Why? What's the matter?
What have I done to her, my maidens, tell me!

HIGH PRIESTESS

Are you considering—?

MEROË

You still intend—?

PENTHESILEA

Nothing, but nothing that should anger her.—
To roll the Ida Mountains up Mount Ossa,
And calmly set myself on top, that's all.

HIGH PRIESTESS

To roll the Ida—?

MEROË

Roll them up Mount Ossa?

PROTHOË [*turning away*]

Protect her, mighty gods on high!

HIGH PRIESTESS

She's lost!

MEROË [*shyly*]

That is an exercise for giants, my Queen!

PENTHESILEA
True, true: but wherein do I yield to them?
MEROË
Wherein you yield to——?
PROTHOË
                    Heaven!
HIGH PRIESTESS
                              But assuming——?
MEROË
Assuming you could carry out this task——?
PROTHOË
Assuming that, what would you——?
PENTHESILEA
                              Imbeciles!
I'd take him by his flaming hair of gold
And pull him down to me——
PROTHOË
                    Whom?
PENTHESILEA
                              Helios,
As he comes soaring close above my head!

[*The* PRINCESSES *look at each other, speechless and horrified.*]

HIGH PRIESTESS
Drag her away by force!
PENTHESILEA [*looking down into the river*]
                    I must be mad!
Why, there he lies, right at my feet! Take me——

[*She tries to jump into the river;* PROTHOË *and* MEROË *hold her back.*]

PROTHOË
Poor miserable thing.
MEROË
                    She's sinking, lifeless,

Just like a falling garment in our hands.

PRIESTESS [*on the hill*]

Achilles is upon us, Princesses!
The whole array of maidens cannot stop him!

AN AMAZON

You gods! Save her! Protect the maidens' Queen
Against his insolence!

HIGH PRIESTESS [*to the* PRIESTESSES]

Come! Come away!
The thick of battle's not the place for us.

[*Exit* HIGH PRIESTESS *with the* PRIESTESSES
and ROSE MAIDENS.]

SCENE TEN

[*Enter a band of* A M A Z O N S *with bows in their hands.*]

F I R S T   A M A Z O N   [*into the wings*]
Stand back, audacious fool!
S E C O N D   A M A Z O N
                He doesn't hear us.
T H I R D   A M A Z O N
Princesses, if we're not allowed to shoot him,
There's nothing to hold back his mad advance!
S E C O N D   A M A Z O N
What can we do? Speak, Prothoë!
P R O T H O Ë   [*tending to the* Q U E E N]
                Then shoot
Ten thousand arrows over him!—
    M E R O Ë   [*to the retinue of* P R I N C E S S E S]
                Some water!
P R O T H O Ë
Take care, though, not to kill him with your shots!—
M E R O Ë
I said, bring water in a helmet!
    A   P R I N C E S S   [*She fills a helmet with water from the
river and brings it.*]
                Here!
T H I R D   A M A Z O N   [*to* P R O T H O Ë]
We won't! Don't worry!
F I R S T   A M A Z O N
              Take up positions here!
Aim but to graze his cheeks and scorch his locks,
Give him the kiss of death to taste in passing!

[*They ready their bows.*]

66

SCENE ELEVEN

[ACHILLES *without helmet, armor, or weapons, followed by several* GREEKS]

ACHILLES
Well, maidens, who's the target for these arrows?
I trust it's not this unprotected breast?
Shall I tear off for you this silken shirt
To show the harmless beating of my heart?
        FIRST AMAZON
Remove it, if you like!
        SECOND AMAZON
                        No, there's no need!
        THIRD AMAZON
Aim straight at where he holds his hand right now!
        FIRST AMAZON
And make his heart fly spitted on the shaft
Just like some windblown leaf—
        MEROË
                        Strike! Shoot!

[*They shoot over his head.*]

        ACHILLES
                                Leave off!
Your eyes are better aimed than all these arrows.
By the Olympians, I don't speak in jest,
I have been wounded deep inside, I feel it,
And as a man disarmed, in every sense,
I lay myself before your little feet.
        FIFTH AMAZON [*struck by a javelin from offstage*]
Merciful gods!

[*She falls.*]

SIXTH AMAZON [*likewise*]
Oh grief!

[*She falls.*]

SEVENTH AMAZON [*likewise*]
Oh Artemis!

[*She falls.*]

FIRST AMAZON
He's raving mad!
MEROË [*busy with the Queen*]   [*together*]
How I do pity her!

SECOND AMAZON
He calls himself disarmed!
PROTHOË [*likewise*]   [*together*]
Her soul has left her.

THIRD AMAZON
And all the while his soldiers overwhelm us!
MEROË   [*together*]
And all our maidens sinking to the ground!
What's to be done?

FIRST AMAZON
The sickle-bladed car!
SECOND AMAZON
The pack of dogs!

THIRD AMAZON
Atop the elephant towers
Pelt him with stones from all sides till he's buried!
AMAZON PRINCESS [*suddenly leaving the* QUEEN]
All right, I'll settle matters with a shot.

[*She unslings her bow and draws it.*]

ACHILLES [*addressing various* AMAZONS *in turn*]
I don't believe it: sweet, like sounding silver,
Your bell-like voices give your words the lie.

You with the blue eyes, you are not the one
To set flesh-tearing hounds on me, nor you,
In the soft splendor of your silky hair.
Consider, if you rashly gave the signal,
And they, let off the leash, came howling by,
You would leap in between, you'd make a shield
Of your own bodies to protect this heart,
This manly heart that glows with love for you.

FIRST AMAZON

The insolent!

SECOND AMAZON

    Just listen to him boasting!

FIRST AMAZON

He thinks with flattering words he can—

THIRD AMAZON [*calling secretly to the first*]

        Oterpe!

FIRST AMAZON [*turning around*]

Ha, look at her! The best of all our archers!
Quietly open up your ranks!

FIFTH AMAZON

      What for?

FOURTH AMAZON

Don't ask! Just wait and see.

EIGHTH AMAZON

      Here! Take this arrow!

AMAZON PRINCESS [*fitting the arrow on the bow*]

I'm going to pin his thighs together with it.

ACHILLES [*to a* GREEK *who, standing beside him,
has already drawn his bow*]

Get her!

AMAZON PRINCESS

  Olympians!

[*She falls.*]

FIRST AMAZON

    The man's a horror!

SECOND AMAZON

It's she who's hit and falls!

THIRD AMAZON

Gods everlasting!
Another band of Greeks is drawing near!

[*Enter* D I O M E D E S *and the* E T O L I A N S *from the other side of the stage. Soon after,* O D Y S S E U S *enters from Achilles' side with the army.*]

D I O M E D E S
This way, my brave Etolians, follow me!

[*He leads them across the bridge.*]

P R O T H O Ë
Oh holy Artemis our goddess! Help!
This is the end for all of us!

[*With the help of several* A M A Z O N S *she carries the* Q U E E N *to the front of the stage.*]

T H E   A M A Z O N S   [*bewildered*]
                        We're trapped!
They're all around us now! We've been cut off!
Run! Save yourself whoever can!
        D I O M E D E S   [*to* P R O T H O Ë]
                        Surrender!
        M E R O Ë   [*to the fleeing* A M A Z O N S]
Have you gone mad? What is this? Stand and fight!
Prothoë! Look!
        P R O T H O Ë   [*still with the* Q U E E N]
                    Away! Run after them,
And if you can, come back and set us free.

[*The* A M A Z O N S *disperse.* M E R O Ë *follows them.*]

A C H I L L E S
She's tall, my friends. Who sees her head?
        A   G R E E K
                                Right there!

ACHILLES
I'll give ten crowns to Diomede for this.
DIOMEDES
I say it again, surrender!
PROTHOË
                        Not to you!
I shall surrender her to him who won her!
Who are you, anyway? She's his, Achilles'!
DIOMEDES [to the ETOLIANS]
Then knock her down!
AN ETOLIAN
                        Attack!
ACHILLES [pushing back the ETOLIAN]
                        He leaves this place
A shadow who lays hand upon the Queen!—
She's mine! Away! What business have you here—
DIOMEDES
Yours! Really! By Zeus the thunderer's locks,
What are your reasons, pray? And with what right?
ACHILLES
One reason on the right, one on the left.—
Give.
PROTHOË
     Here. From your great heart I need fear nothing.
ACHILLES [taking the QUEEN into his arms]
Nothing.—

          [To DIOMEDES]

          Go give the women chase and beat them;
I'll stay behind with her a moment. Off!
Do it for me. Don't argue. I would fight
Hades himself for her sake, why not you?

          [He lays her down against the root of an oak tree.]

          DIOMEDES
So be it! Follow me!

ODYSSEUS [*crossing the stage with the army*]
                    Well done, Achilles!
Your thundering war car, shall I fetch it for you?
        ACHILLES [*bent over the* QUEEN]
No need for it. Not yet.
        ODYSSEUS
                        Good. As you will.—
Now follow me! Before the women rally.

        [*Exit* ODYSSEUS *and* DIOMEDES *with the army, on
        the Amazons' side of the stage.*]

[PENTHESILEA, PROTHOË, ACHILLES, GREEKS, *and*
AMAZONS *in attendance*]

ACHILLES [*opening the* QUEEN's *armor*]
She's not alive.
          PROTHOË
          Oh I do wish her eyes
Were closed forever to this desolate light!
I'm all too fearful that she will awake.
          ACHILLES
Where was she hit?
          PROTHOË
               She rallied from your blow,
Which tore her breast, by sheerest force of will;
And to this place we led her, staggering,
And were about to climb that rock with her.
But, for what reason I can't say, the pain
Of wounded limbs, of injury to her soul:
She could not bear that you had won against her;
Her foot refused to serve her, and gave way,
And, babbling senseless words with pallid lips,
She fell a second time into my arms.
          ACHILLES
She quivered—did you see?
          PROTHOË
               Heavenly gods!
Has she not emptied out her cup of sorrows?
Look down upon her suffering—
          ACHILLES
               She's breathing.
          PROTHOË
Oh son of Peleus! If you know pity,
If just one feeling stirs within your breast,
If you do not intend to kill her or

Enmesh her high-strung nerves in lunacy,
I beg you, grant me this one wish.

ACHILLES

Speak quickly!

PROTHOË

Leave! Leave this place, most excellent, noble Prince,
And from her sight withdraw when she awakes.
Straightway remove the troop that stands around you,
And let not anyone, before the sun
Renews his light in far-off mountain vapors,
Approach and greet her with the deadly words:
You are Achilles' prisoner of war.

ACHILLES

She hates me, then?

PROTHOË

Oh do not ask, great heart!—
If joyfully, led by the hand of hope,
She now returns to life, let not the victor
Be the first joyless view that meets her eye.
How many a thing moves in a woman's breast
That was not fashioned for the light of day.
If in the end, as destiny demands,
She must in pain salute you as your captive,
Do not insist upon it, I implore you,
Until her spirit has put on its armor.

ACHILLES

My will, I have to tell you, is to treat her
Just as I did King Priam's haughty son.

PROTHOË

What was that, monster!

ACHILLES

—Is she afraid of that?

PROTHOË

You would inflict the unspeakable upon her?
This youthful body here, you man of horrors,
Adorned with beauties like a child with flowers,
You mean to drag it, like a corpse, in shame—?

ACHILLES

Tell her I love her.

PROTHOË

What?— What did you—? How—?

ACHILLES

How? By the gods above! As men love women;
Chastely, and yet with longing; in innocence,
Yet eager to deprive her of her own.
I want to take her for my wedded queen.

PROTHOË

Gods everlasting, say those words again.
You want—?

ACHILLES

Now can I stay?

PROTHOË

Oh let me kiss
Your feet, god among men! Oh now if you
Were gone, unto the Pillars of Hercules
I'd go to find you, son of Peleus!
But look: her eyes are opening—

ACHILLES

She's moving—

PROTHOË

It's now or never! Men, go off; and you,
Take cover, quick, behind this oak tree—hurry!

ACHILLES

Away, my friends! Retreat.

[*Exit Achilles' retinue.*]

PROTHOË [*To* ACHILLES, *as he steps behind an oak*]

Go deeper yet!
And I beseech you, do not show your face
Until I call you. Will you promise that?
Her soul cannot be reckoned with, believe me.

ACHILLES

It shall be so.

PROTHOË

Now then, pay close attention!

SCENE FOURTEEN

[PENTHESILEA, PROTHOË, ACHILLES, *and* AMAZONS
in attendance]

PROTHOË

Penthesilea! Where have you been, oh dreamer!
In what far fields of radiance does your spirit
Still soar and sweep, with restless beating wings,
As if it were displeased with its own home,
The while your happy fate, like a young prince,
Seeks lodging in your bosom and, surprised
To find such lovely habitation empty,
Turns round again and wends his fleeting steps
Already back to heaven whence he came?
Will you not bind this guest, my foolish friend?—
Come, raise yourself, lean on my breast.

PENTHESILEA

                                   Where am I?

PROTHOË

Do you not know your sister's voice? That cliff,
This path across the bridge, this blooming landscape,
Do none of these recall you to yourself?
Look at these maidens gathered round about you.
As if before the portals of a world
More fair than ours, they stand and bid you welcome.
—You sigh. What are you afraid of?

PENTHESILEA

                                   Prothoë!

Oh what a dream of horror I have dreamt.
How sweet it is, it makes me long for tears,
To wake and feel my heart, so tired of torment,
Beating against this sister heart of yours—
—I dreamt that in the whirling tide of battle
The son of Peleus struck me with his lance;

Amidst the clatter of my brazen armor,
I fell; the earth resounded with the crash.
And while the army, in dismay, shrinks back—
I'm still cast down with all my limbs entangled—
He swings himself already from his horse,
And strides, with steps of triumph, toward me,
And now he grips me, helpless as I lie there,
With powerful arms he lifts me from the ground,
I try and try in vain to grasp this dagger,
I am a prisoner, with mockery
And laughter I am taken to his tents.

            PROTHOË
Not so, my dearest Queen! His kingly soul
Is too magnanimous for mockery.
If what you dreamt were living truth: believe me,
A blessed moment would have been your lot,
And prostrate in the dust you might have seen
The son of men and gods, adoring you.

            PENTHESILEA
Accursed if I should live to see the shame!
Accursed if ever I receive a man
Not honorably conquered with a sword!

            PROTHOË
Be calm, my Queen.

            PENTHESILEA
                        Be calm! Why should I be—

            PROTHOË
Are you not resting on my faithful bosom?
Whatever fate impends upon you now,
We will endure together: calm yourself.

            PENTHESILEA
I was as peaceful, Prothoë, as the sea
That nestles in a rocky cove; not one
Emotion rose in waves to trouble me.
These words: be calm! now churn me up like wind
Lashing the open waters of the world.
What is there that requires my being calm?
You stand so strange about me, so disturbed—
—And casting looks, by the eternal gods,

Not so, my dearest Queen! His kingly soul
Is too magnanimous for mockery

Behind my back, as if a monster stood
With wild demeanor threatening behind me.
—I tell you, it was just a dream, it isn't—
Or is it? No? Could it be real? Speak!—
—Where's Meroë? And Megaris?

[*She looks around and sees* ACHILLES.]

                        Oh gods!
There, there he is, the horror, right behind me!
But now with my free hand—

[*She draws her dagger.*]

PROTHOË
                        Unhappy soul!
PENTHESILEA
The worthless wretch, she tries to hinder me—
PROTHOË
Achilles, save her!
PENTHESILEA
                    Have you lost your senses!
He's come to plant his foot upon my neck!
PROTHOË
His foot? You're mad—
PENTHESILEA
                        Away from me, I say!—
PROTHOË
Why don't you look at him, you poor lost thing—!
Does he not stand behind you without weapons?
PENTHESILEA
What's that?
PROTHOË
            Why, yes! Prepared, if you so wish it,
To take upon himself your garland-fetters.
PENTHESILEA
No, speak!
PROTHOË
Achilles! Speak! She won't believe me.

PENTHESILEA
My prisoner—he?

PROTHOË
                    How else! It's clear enough!

ACHILLES [*who has meanwhile stepped forward*]
In every nobler sense, exalted Queen,
Prepared henceforth to flutter out my life
A captive bound and fettered by your eyes.

[PENTHESILEA *covers her face with both hands.*]

PROTHOË
Well, there it is, you've heard it from his lips.
—He, when you met, sank with you to the dust;
And while you lay unconscious on the ground
He was disarmed—weren't you?

ACHILLES
                              I was disarmed.
And then conducted here before your feet.

[*He bends his knee before her.*]

PENTHESILEA [*after a brief pause*]
If that be so, I welcome you, fresh charm
Of life, young god with roses in your cheeks!
And now, my heart, release the stagnant blood
That waits, as if attending his arrival,
Heaped up within both chambers of my breast.
You wingèd couriers of untrammeled joy,
Sweet liquors of my youth, spring forth and fly
With all your might rejoicing through my veins,
And let the message, like a crimson flag,
Be flown through all the kingdoms of this face:
The young son of the Nereid is mine!

[*She stands up.*]

PROTHOË
Do temper yourself, please, my precious Queen.

PENTHESILEA [*stepping forward*]

Now come, you maidens crowned with victory,
Daughters of Mars, still covered with the dust
Of war from head to toe, come unto me,
Each leading by the hand the Argive youth
She conquered on the field of mortal combat!
You rose-girls with your baskets, come, step nearer:
It seems we have more brows than garlands here!
Go out, and scan the fields again, I say,
Search for those roses which the spring withholds
And coax them from the meadows with your breath!
Priestesses of Diana, rouse yourselves:
Your temple filled with light and frankincense,
Let all its doors fly open with a clangor
As if they were the gates of Paradise!
First lead the bull, well fattened, short of horn,
Before the altar; fell him with a flash
Of iron, soundless in that holy place
But for the rafters shaking at his fall.
You servants of the temple, stout, strong-limbed,
The blood! Where are you? Busy yourselves, quick,
With Persian oils still hissing from the coals,
To wipe the paneled surface clean of it.
And all you fluttering garments, gird yourselves,
You golden beakers, fill yourselves with wine,
You trumpets, blare, resound, you mighty horns,
And let the noise of your melodious joy
Send tremors to the very vault of heaven!—
Oh Prothoë! Help me rejoice, exult!
Invent for me, friend, sister heart, imagine
How I might make a feast more heavenly,
More godlike than the revels of Olympus,
The wedding feast of brides in battle wooed,
Mars' daughters and the sons of Inachos!
Oh Meroë, where are you? Megaris?

PROTHOË [*moved, but suppressing her emotion*]

Both joy and grief are ruinous to you,
One drives you mad as surely as the other.
You dream, *dream* that you're back in Themiscyra,

And when your longing flies beyond all limits,
I'm sorely tempted with a well-aimed word
To paralyze your wings and force you down.
Just look about, deluded Queen, where are you?
Where are your people? Where the priestesses?
Asteria? Meroë? Megaris? Where are they?

PENTHESILEA [*leaning on her breast*]
Oh let me, Prothoë! Oh let this heart
Dive under, like a sullied child, and bathe
Two minutes in this stream of limpid joy!
With every stroke beneath its bounteous waves
A blemish from my heart is washed away.
The cruel Eumenides have taken flight,
I feel the wafting nearness of the gods,
And right away I want to join their choir,
Never was I so ripe for death as now.
But now, above all else: you do forgive me?

PROTHOË
My sovereign ruler!

PENTHESILEA
                              Yes, I know, I know.—
Yours is the better portion of my blood.
—They say misfortune purifies the spirit,
But I, beloved, I have not found it so;
I feel but bitterness, and passionate,
Unfathomable spite at gods and men.
How strangely hateful was in every face
The look of joy to me, whenever I saw it;
The child at play upon its mother's lap
Seemed a conspirator against my pain.
And now, how gladly all the world around me
Would I see happy and content. Ah, friend!
We can be great in suffering, heroic,
But like the gods are those who dwell in bliss!
—But let's attend to business. Have the army
Make all arrangements for a swift return;
As soon as the battalions, maid and beast,
Are rested, we'll guide the train of prisoners
Back to the meadows of our native land.

—Where is Lykaon?

PROTHOË

                      Who?

PENTHESILEA [*with tender reproach*]
                      How can you ask?
The Arcadian hero in the flower of youth—
You took him with your sword. Whatever is keeping him?

PROTHOË [*confused*]
He is still waiting in the woods, my Queen!
Where all the other captives are being held.
Please grant that he, according to the law,
Not come before me till we have returned.

PENTHESILEA
Have him brought here! —Still waiting in the woods!
—Here at my Prothoë's feet is where he should be!
——I beg you, please, dear heart, do have him called.
You stand beside me like a frost in May,
And hem the nascent life of joy within me.

PROTHOË [*aside*]
Poor fated creature! —Very well, then, go
And carry out your sovereign Queen's command.

[*She motions to an* AMAZON, *who exits.*]

PENTHESILEA
Now who will go and fetch the rose-girls for me?

[*She sees roses lying on the ground.*]

Oh look! Blossoms, and such sweet-smelling ones,
Are to be found right here—!

[*She passes her hand across her forehead.*]

                      My evil dream!

[*To* PROTHOË]

Was the High Priestess of Diana here?

PROTHOË

Not that I can remember, gracious Queen.

PENTHESILEA

How did the roses get here, then?

PROTHOË [*hastily*]

Look here!
The rose-girls who went out to scour the fields
Seem to have left a basketful behind.
Now this, I'd say, is a timely stroke of chance.
Here, let me gather up these fragrant blossoms
And wind the Peleid's garland for you. Shall I?

[*She sits down by the oak tree.*]

PENTHESILEA

My darling! Precious sister! How you move me.—
All right! And these here, with a hundred petals,
I'll wind you for Lykaon's wreath. Come on.

[*She also gathers up some roses, and sits down next to*
PROTHOË.]

Make music, women, music! I'm not calm.
Sing out with your clear voices! Quiet me.

A MAIDEN [*from her retinue*]

What would you like?

ANOTHER MAIDEN

The victory song?

PENTHESILEA

—The hymn.

THE MAIDEN

Very well. —Oh grievously misled! —Sing! Play!

CHORUS OF MAIDENS [*with music*]

Ares departs!
See how his horses all white
Trailing vapors afar to Orcus fly!
They let him in, the fearsome Eumenides:
They close the grim portals shut behind him again.

A MAIDEN
Hymen! Where art thou?
Kindle the torch, and light us! Light us!
Hymen! Where art thou?

CHORUS
Ares departs! [*etc.*]

ACHILLES [*secretly approaches* PROTHOË *during the song*]
Where will this take me? Speak! I want to know!

PROTHOË
Just one brief moment more, greathearted soul,
I beg you to be patient. You will see.

[*When the garlands are wound,* PENTHESILEA *exchanges hers for* PROTHOË *'s; they embrace and look at the wreaths. The music stops. The* AMAZON *returns.*]

PENTHESILEA
You've carried out my order?

AMAZON
                                  Young Lykaon,
Prince of Arcadia, will appear forthwith.

SCENE FIFTEEN

[PENTHESILEA, PROTHOË, ACHILLES, AMAZONS]

PENTHESILEA

Now come, you sweet son of the Nereid,
Come close, lie down here at my feet— Still closer!
Be bold! ——Surely you're not afraid of me?
—Or hate me for defeating you? Speak out!
Do you fear her who laid you in the dust?

ACHILLES

Fear her? As flowers fear sunshine.

PENTHESILEA

                              Nicely said!
Then look upon me as your source of light.—
Diana! Ruler of my days, he has
A wound!

ACHILLES

          A scratch upon my arm, no more.

PENTHESILEA

I beg you, Peleid, do not believe
That I have ever aimed to take your life.
True, with this arm here I was glad to strike you,
But when I saw you sinking down, my breast
Was envious of the dust that would receive you.

ACHILLES

If you love me, you'll speak of this no more.
See, it is healing.

PENTHESILEA

                  Then you do forgive me?

ACHILLES

Of course. With all my heart.—

PENTHESILEA

                              Now—can you tell me:

How does Love, being but a small wingèd boy,
Tame the defiant lion and tether him?
ACHILLES
I think he must caress his bristly cheeks.
Then he'll hold still.
PENTHESILEA
                    In that case, I believe
You'll stir no more than does a fledgling dove
Around whose neck a young girl lays a sling.
Because the feelings in this breast, oh youth,
Are just like hands, and are caressing you.

[*She winds garlands around him.*]

ACHILLES
Who are you, wondrous woman?
PENTHESILEA
                    There, don't move.—
Hold still, I said! You'll find out very soon.
—Only this light and winding wreath of roses
Around your temples, back behind your neck—
Down to your arms, your hands, your legs, your feet—
Up to your head again——and now it's done.
What are you breathing?
ACHILLES
                    The breath of your sweet lips.
PENTHESILEA [*bending backward*]
It's just the roses scattering their scent.
—No, no!
ACHILLES
          I thought I'd try them at the stem.
PENTHESILEA
As soon as they are ripe, my love, you'll pluck them.

[*She puts another wreath on his head and lets him go.*]

Now it is done. —Oh look, Prothoë, see
How well the melting flush of roses suits him!

How they light up the storm clouds in his face!
Truly, my dearest friend, when from the mountains
Thallo and Carpo lead the newborn day
To his first steps on fields of sparkling diamonds:
His gaze is not so soft and mild as this.—
Speak! Do his eyes not seem alight to you?—
I swear, you'd almost doubt, to see him this way,
That it is he.
                    PROTHOË
                         Who, pray?
            PENTHESILEA
                              The Peleid!—
The one that slew King Priam's greatest son
Before the walls of Troy—speak! Was it you?
And was it you, *you*, who, with these hands, drove
A wedge through that swift foot and dragged him headlong,
Tied to your axle, around his father's city?
Speak! Talk! What moves you so? What is the matter?
            ACHILLES
I am the one.
            PENTHESILEA [*after scrutinizing him*]
                    He says it's he.
            PROTHOË
                              It is.
This ornament is proof of it, my Queen.
            PENTHESILEA
How so?
            PROTHOË
                    Because, see here, this is the armor
That Thetis, his immortal mother, won
By flattery from the god of fire, Hephaestos.
            PENTHESILEA
Then I salute you with this kiss, of human
Beings the most unbridled, mine! It is I,
Young god of war, to whom you now belong!
And when the people ask, you shall name *me*.
            ACHILLES
Oh you who come to me, a dazzling vision

—*Only this light and winding wreath of roses*
Around your temples, back behind your neck—
Down to your arms, your hands, your legs, your feet—
Up to your head again———and now it's done

Descended from above as from the realms
Of ether, unfathomable being, who are you?
How shall I name you when my own soul asks
In ravishment to whom she now belongs?

PENTHESILEA

When your soul asks you that, name her these features:
These be the name by which you think of me.—
For though I give to you this golden ring,
Whose every mark can lend you full assurance,
And will, if you but show it, lead you to me,
A ring is sometimes lost, a name forgotten;
If you forgot the name, or lost the ring:
Would you still find my image in yourself?
Can you still see me when you shut your eyes?

ACHILLES

Engraved as firm as facets in a diamond.

PENTHESILEA

Then know I am the Queen of Amazons;
Of Mars begotten is my ancient tribe,
The famed Otrerë was my noble mother,
Myself the people call: Penthesilea.

ACHILLES

Penthesilea.

PENTHESILEA

          Yes, so I did say.

ACHILLES

My swan in death shall sing: Penthesilea.

PENTHESILEA

I grant you liberty, you may set foot
Within the maidens' camp wherever you please.
For there's another chain I still intend
To wrap around your heart and bind you with,
As light as flowers, more durable than bronze.
But till it has been forged, link within link,
In ardent love and glowing tenderness,
Proof against every strain of time and chance,
You shall return to me, as duty bids you,
To me, young friend, who, hear me well, shall tend

To every need of yours, and every wish.
Tell me, will you return?

    ACHILLES

                              Like a young horse
Drawn to the fragrant oats that feed his life.

    PENTHESILEA

Good. I will take you at your word. And now
We must be on our way to Themiscyra;
Till we are there, my stable is all yours.
You shall be housed in purple canopies;
Nor shall you lack for slaves to do your bidding
And carry out your every kingly wish.
But since, you understand, the march will claim
Much thought of me and many a care, your place
For now will be among the other captives:
In Themiscyra, then, with all my heart
I shall be doting on you, son of Thetis.

    ACHILLES

It shall be so.

    PENTHESILEA [to PROTHOË]

                   But tell me, Prothoë,
Where is your young Arcadian?

    PROTHOË

                              Oh my Queen—

    PENTHESILEA

I'll be so glad, beloved friend, to see him
Crowned by your hand.

    PROTHOË

                      I'm sure he'll be here soon.—
This garland here shall crown him without fail.

    PENTHESILEA [making motions to leave]

Well, then— I have much business to attend to,
So let me go.

    ACHILLES

              What?

    PENTHESILEA

                  Let me rise, my friend.

    ACHILLES

You're going away? You're leaving me behind?

Before disclosing to my longing heart
These many wonders I have seen, my love?

PENTHESILEA

In Themiscyra, friend.

ACHILLES

                    Please, here, my Queen!

PENTHESILEA

In Themiscyra, friend, in Themiscyra—
Let go now!

PROTHOË [*holding her back, agitated*]
          What? My Queen! Where are you going?

PENTHESILEA [*puzzled*]
I'm leaving to review the armies—strange!
And speak with Meroë and Megaris.
There's more to do, by Zeus, than stand and talk!

PROTHOË

Our troops are giving chase to the Greek army.—
Meroë's in charge, so leave the worry to her;
You still need rest. And once the enemy
Has pulled back all the way across Scamander,
You'll see our victory parade right here.

PENTHESILEA [*thinking it over*]
Oh? ——Here, on this field? Are you quite sure?

PROTHOË

Quite sure. You can rely on it.

PENTHESILEA [*to* ACHILLES]
                    Be brief, then.

ACHILLES

How is it, wondrous woman, that, like Pallas,
Galloping at the head of a fierce army,
You should fall suddenly, as from a cloud,
And unprovoked, into our fight with Troy?
What is it that incites you, dressed in bronze
From head to foot, and like a Fury filled
With blinding rage, against the tribes of Greece;
You who need but serenely show yourself
In all your loveliness to see the race
Of men kneel down before you in the dust?

PENTHESILEA

Alas! Son of the Nereid! To me
That gentler art of women was not granted.
Not at the games, like daughters of your country,
When in great streams the pride and glory of youth
Come from afar to vie in joyful contest,
May I seek out the one I love among them;
Not by arranging flowers this way or that,
Or with averted eyes attract his notice;
Not in a nightingale-enchanted grove
Of pomegranates in the glow of dawn
Lean on his breast and tell him he's the one.
On bloody battlegrounds I have to seek him,
The youth my heart has chosen for its own,
And this soft breast may not receive him sooner
Than I have captured him with arms of bronze.

ACHILLES

What place, what time could issue such a law,
Unfeminine, forgive me, unnatural,
So foreign to all other tribes and nations?

PENTHESILEA

It issued from the urn of the most holy,
Oh youth: it came from far, from peaks of time,
Untrod by any man, which heaven has
Forever veiled in clouds of mystery.
The word of our first mothers did decree it,
And it commands our silence, son of Thetis,
As your first fathers' word commands your own.

ACHILLES

Speak plainer.

PENTHESILEA

          Very well! Then listen closely.—
Where now the Amazonian nation rules,
There lived before, obedient to the gods,
Warlike and free, a tribe of Scythians,
Equal to any nation on the earth.
For many centuries this race had named
The flower-embosomed Caucasus their own:
When Vexoris, the Ethiopian King,

Appeared among the foothills, swiftly threw
The tribesmen, joined in battle, down before him,
Poured through the valleys, cutting down old men
And boys, wherever his cruel sword could reach:
And with them died the splendor of the world.
The victors insolently set up house
In our own huts and, as barbarians will,
Fed themselves on the fruit of our rich fields,
And, to allot us our full measure of shame,
Forced us to tender them a loving welcome:
They tore the women from their husbands' graves,
And dragged them off to share their loathsome beds.

ACHILLES

It was a devastating fate indeed,
My Queen, that brought your women's state to life.

PENTHESILEA

But human nature, pressed beyond endurance,
Rebels and shakes the burden from its back;
Afflictions must be moderate to be borne.
For nights on end, in secrecy and silence,
The women lay in Ares' temple, praying for
Salvation, hollowing the steps with tears.
The desecrated beds began to fill
With daggers, sharp-edged wedges cut and shaped
From ornaments, in secret by the hearth,
From spangles, buckles, rings; only the wedding
Of Vexoris, the Ethiopian King,
And young Tanaïs, the Queen, delayed the kiss
Each held in keeping for her captor's breast.
And when at last the wedding feast had come,
Tanaïs plunged her knife into his heart,
Mars in his stead carried out the marriage rite,
And in a night the murderers had their itch
Well satisfied, with knives, till they were dead.

ACHILLES

I can believe the women would have done that.

PENTHESILEA

The people's council made a proclamation:
Free as the wind upon the fallow plains

Are women who have acted with such valor,
And shall no longer serve the race of men.
Hence let there be a sovereign nation founded,
A state of women where the arrogant,
Imperious voice of man shall not be heard;
That gives itself its laws in dignity,
Obeys itself, provides its own protection:
And brave Tanaïs shall be empowered as Queen.
And should a man set eye upon this nation,
That eye shall be forever closed again;
And should it happen that an infant boy
Be born of tyrant blood, dispatch him straight
To Orcus, where his savage fathers went.
Now Ares' temple filled at once with throngs
Who came to see the great Tanaïs crowned
Protectress of a state so constituted.
But at the solemn moment when she mounted
The altar steps, where the High Priestess stood,
Adorned in splendor, with the mighty bow,
The golden emblem of the power of kings
Who theretofore had governed Scythia,
And reached out to receive it, a voice spoke:
"A state like this will be the laughingstock
Of men, no more than that, and at the first
Attack of warlike neighbors, it will crumble:
Because a woman hampered by full breasts,
And weak, can never learn to draw a bow,
And loose its power, as easily as a man."
The Queen, Tanaïs, stood silent for a moment
To see what fortune such a speech might find;
But as the crowd shrank back in craven fear,
She tore off her right breast, and baptized those
Whose task it was to wield the bow and arrow,
And fell into a faint before she'd finished:
The Amazons, that is, the Bosomless!—
And then the crown was set upon her head.
        ACHILLES
By Zeus the thunderer, she didn't *need* breasts!

94

That woman could have ruled a race of men;
With all my heart and soul I bow to her.

PENTHESILEA

Upon that deed a silence fell, Achilles.
Only the whirring of the bow was heard,
As it dropped from the deathly pale, stiff hands
Of the High Priestess to the temple floor.
It dropped, the Empire's giant, golden bow,
And clanged against the marble steps three times
With a resounding drone, like a huge bell,
And lay, silent as death, before her feet.—

ACHILLES

I hope that in your motherland the women
Don't follow her example.

PENTHESILEA

                              No—they don't!
Not with a zeal comparable to hers.

ACHILLES

What! Then you do—? Impossible!

PENTHESILEA

                              How so?—

ACHILLES

Then it is true, this monstrous tale we've heard?
And all this loveliness surrounding you,
These shining girls, the flower of womanhood,
So gracefully decked out, each one a perfect
Altar to kneel before in adoration,
Are wantonly, inhumanly, deprived—?

PENTHESILEA

You didn't know about this?

ACHILLES [pressing his face to her bosom]
                              Oh my Queen!
The seat of kindness, tenderness, and youth,
For this barbaric lunacy—

PENTHESILEA

                              Don't worry.
Those feelings all found refuge over here,
Where they dwell all the nearer to the heart.

I trust of these you won't find any lacking.
ACHILLES
I swear! I've had dreams at the break of dawn
That seemed to me more truthful than this moment.
—Go on, though.
PENTHESILEA
                    What?
ACHILLES
                              You've not yet told the end.
For if this overly proud women's nation
Was founded without help from men, unless
Men help, how does it propagate itself?
Or does Deucalion still, from time to time,
Toss down one of his clods headfirst among you?
PENTHESILEA
Whenever, after yearly calculations,
The Queen wants to restore the numbers lost
To death, she will select among the women
The ones in fairest bloom—

[*She halts and looks at him.*]

                              You smile?
ACHILLES
                                        Who? I?
PENTHESILEA
I think you're smiling, dearest.
ACHILLES
                              At your beauty.
Forgive me, I was distracted. I was wondering
If you had come down from the moon to meet me.
PENTHESILEA [*after a pause*]
Whenever, after yearly calculations,
The Queen wants to recover for the state
What death has taken from her, she will send
For women from all corners of the realm,
Young and in fairest bloom, and in the temple
Of Artemis in Themiscyra pray

That Ares bless their wombs with fruitfulness.
This Feast of Maids in Bloom—that is its name—
Is celebrated softly and in quiet;
We wait till Nature sheds her snowy garment
And Spring has pressed his lips upon her breast.
After this prayer, Diana's holy Priestess
Betakes herself to Mars, and in his temple,
Prostrate before the altar, begs the god
To grant the wishes of our nation's mother.
The god, then, if he's graciously inclined—
For often he is not; our snowy mountains
Do not yield nourishment too readily—
The god makes known to us, through his High Priestess,
A people, chaste and lordly, who will soon
Appear to us in his stead, as his proxy.
That people's name and dwelling place pronounced,
A great rejoicing spreads through town and country.
The maids are glorified as brides of Mars,
They receive gifts of weapons from their mothers,
Arrows and dagger, and over all their limbs
There flies, amid a joyful flurry of
Attendant hands, the wedding dress of bronze.
The glad day of departure is then set,
The muted trumpets sound, the band of girls
Leap, whispering, onto their horses' backs,
And stealthily, as if on woolen soles,
Advance through shining nights, through wood and valley,
To the far camp of the divinely chosen.
That land once reached, we halt before its gates,
And rest for two whole days, both troops and horses:
Then, like a fire-blazing storm, we burst
Into the forest of men and whirl about,
And waft the ripest of the ones that fall,
Like seeds dropped from the crowns of clashing trees,
Off to the meadows of our native land.
Here, in Diana's temple, we attend them
Through many a holy rite, of which the name
Alone is known to me: the Feast of Roses—

And which, on pain of death, may not be approached
Except by the victorious brides themselves—
Until the seed has blossomed in our wombs;
Then shower them with presents, each, like kings;
And at the Feast of Ripeness send them home
On horses gorgeously caparisoned.
This festival, alas, is not the gladdest,
Son of the Nereid—there is much weeping,
And many a heart is seized with dismal sorrow,
And cannot grasp why every utterance should
Begin with praises of the great Tanaïs.
What are you dreaming?

ACHILLES

                            I?

PENTHESILEA

                                      Yes, you.

ACHILLES

                                                My love,
More than I could express in words right now.
———Do you intend to send me home like that?

PENTHESILEA

I don't know, dear. Don't ask me this.—

ACHILLES

                                              How strange!

[*He ponders.*]

But one more revelation you will grant me.

PENTHESILEA

Gladly, my friend. Be bold.

ACHILLES

                            What is the reason
You gave such hot pursuit to me alone?
It seemed as if you knew me.

PENTHESILEA

                                So I did.

ACHILLES

But how?

PENTHESILEA
　　You won't smile at my foolishness?
ACHILLES [*smiling*]
I say, as you did: I don't know.
PENTHESILEA
　　　　　　　　　Very well,
I'll tell you. See, I had already witnessed
The Festival of Roses twenty times
And three, and from a distance, where the temple
Rises above a forest of oaks, heard sounds
Of voices crying aloud with joy; when Ares,
After my mother Queen Otrerë's death,
Elected me to be his bride. For we
May not, as princesses of royal blood,
Join in the Festival of Maids in Bloom
Of our own will; but if the god desires us,
We will receive the honor of his call,
Delivered by the lips of his High Priestess.
My mother was expiring in my arms,
Already pale as death, when I was given
The message of the god, a solemn call
To leave the palace and depart for Troy,
And bring him home from there bedecked with garlands.
It happened that no substitute before
Was chosen who so pleased the brides of Mars
As the Hellenic tribes that battled there.
At every corner, voices would exult
In noble songs, on every marketplace,
Praising the deeds of that heroic war:
Of Paris' apple and the rape of Helen,
The sons of Atreus marshaling their hosts,
Of Briseis, the burning of the ships,
And of Patroclus' death, and with what pomp
Of vengeful triumph you paid tribute to him;
And all the deeds and marvels of this time.—
I was dissolved in grief, and could but listen
With half an ear to what those messengers
Had brought me at Otrerë's hour of death:

"My mother, let me stay with you," I cried:
"Employ your royal privilege today
For one last time, and bid these women go."
But in her dignity, the Queen, who long
Had wished to see me on the battlefield—
For she would leave no heirs, and there were kin
Ambitious to succeed her on the throne—
She said: "Go, my sweet child! Ares is calling!
Your garland shall adorn the Peleid's brow:
Become a mother, proud and glad, as I am—"
And gently pressed my hand, and passed away.

    PROTHOË

And so she named him to you, Queen Otrerë?

    PENTHESILEA

She named him, Prothoë, as well a mother
May take her child into her confidence.

    ACHILLES

Why should she not? Or does the law forbid this?

    PENTHESILEA

It is not fitting for a daughter of Mars
To seek out her opponent; she must choose
The one sent by the god to stand against her.—
If in her zeal, however, she shows herself
Before the princeliest foes, so much the better.
—Is that not so, Prothoë?

    PROTHOË

                 It is.

    ACHILLES

                 And then—?

    PENTHESILEA

All through a long, unhappy moon I wept
Before my mother's grave, not even touching
The crown that lay beside it, masterless,
Until the people's oft-repeated cry,
For they were teeming round the palace grounds,
Impatient, ready for the war, tore me
By force onto the throne. So it was with
A mournful and unwilling heart I came

To Ares' temple; the Priestess offered me
The ringing bow of the Amazonian Empire,
I thought I felt my mother's presence near me
As I received it, nothing seemed more sacred
Than to fulfill and honor her last wish.
I strewed flowers, the most fragrant I could find,
On her sarcophagus, and then set forth
With all the armies of the Amazons
To the high walls of Ilium—but less
To please the great god who had sent me there
Than to give solace to Otrerë's shade.

ACHILLES

Sorrow for your dead mother briefly lamed
The strength that usually adorns your breast.

PENTHESILEA

I loved her.

ACHILLES

      Then what happened?

PENTHESILEA

                    Day by day,
As I drew nearer to Scamander's bank,
And heard, in all the valleys I coursed through,
The echoing din of battle before Troy,
My pain began to lessen, and my soul
Awoke to the great world of brilliant war.
I had this thought: If I should see them all,
The grandest moments of past history,
Repeated here, if the whole company
Of mighty heroes praised in songs of old
Descended to me from the stars, I should
Find none more excellent to crown with roses
Than him my mother designated for me,
Beloved and savage, sweet and terrible hero
Who laid great Hector low! Oh son of Peleus!
My one unending thought when I was waking,
My endless dream, was you! The entire world
Lay stretched before me like a patterned web
With wide and ample meshes, and each one

Had one of your deeds woven into it,
And into my heart, white and pure as silk,
I branded each of them with flaming colors.
I all but saw you, by the walls of Troy,
Felling the son of Priam in full flight;
Saw your face turning back, flushed with the high
Delight of victory, while his bloodied head
Dragged on the naked earth behind your horse;
Saw Priam himself come begging to your tent—
And wept hot tears to think that through your breast,
Though hard as marble and devoid of mercy,
A feeling might still find its darting way.
      ACHILLES
Beloved Queen!
      PENTHESILEA
              But how I felt, my friend,
When I set eyes upon your very self—!
When you appeared in the Scamander valley
Surrounded by the heroes of your people,
A day-star among pallid stars of night!
I could not have felt otherwise if he
Himself, the god of war, had of a sudden
Come with his white horses thundering down
From Mount Olympus to salute his bride!
I stood there, dazzled by the apparition,
After you had withdrawn—as, when at night
Lightning falls before a wanderer,
The rumbling portals of Elysium open
With radiance for a soul and close again.
At that same moment, Peleid, I guessed
From where this feeling surged into my bosom:
The god of love had struck me with his arrow.
But quickly I resolved I would accept
But one of these: to win you or to die.
And now the sweeter privilege is mine.
—Why do you stare?

    [*Sound of clashing weapons in the distance*]

PROTHOË [*secretly to* ACHILLES]
                    Son of the gods, I beg you,
You must declare yourself to her at once.
    PENTHESILEA [*starting up*]
Argives are coming, women! Rise!
    ACHILLES [*holding her back*]
                            Be calm!
Those are the sounds of prisoners, my Queen.
    PENTHESILEA
Of prisoners?
    PROTHOË [*secretly to* ACHILLES]
            By the Styx, it is Odysseus!
Your troops, hard-pressed by Meroë, are retreating!
    ACHILLES [*muttering into his beard*]
Would that they turned to stone!
    PENTHESILEA
                        What is it? Tell me!
    ACHILLES [*with forced gaiety*]
Your child, our son, shall be the god of Earth!
Prometheus shall rise up from where he sits
And to the races of the world proclaim:
Here is a man as I would have men be!
But I'll not follow you to Themiscyra,
But rather you, to blooming Phthia, me:
For once my people's war is finished, that's where
I'll take you, caroling for joy, and seat you,
Blessed that I am, upon my fathers' throne.

    [*The sound continues.*]

    PENTHESILEA
What? I don't understand a word!
    THE WOMEN [*agitated*]
                        Almighty gods!
    PROTHOË
Oh son of Thetis! Would you—?
    PENTHESILEA
                        What? What is it?

ACHILLES

Why, nothing, nothing, do not fear, my Queen!
You see, time's pressing, when I tell you now
What is the fate the gods have chosen for you.
True, by the power of love I am your slave,
And I shall wear these bonds forevermore;
By luck of arms, though, you belong to me;
For it was you, my precious friend, who sank
At *my* feet when we fought, not I at yours.

PENTHESILEA [*drawing herself up*]

You monstrous fiend!

ACHILLES

No, please, I beg you, dearest!
Not even Zeus can alter what has happened.
Master yourself, and listen, like a rock,
To what that messenger, unless I'm wrong,
Will bring me in the way of evil tidings.
To you, as you must realize, he brings nothing;
Your fate is sealed for all eternity;
You are my prisoner, a hound of hell
Would guard you less ferociously than I.

PENTHESILEA

Your prisoner, I?

ACHILLES

That's how it is, my Queen!

PENTHESILEA [*raising her hands*]

Eternal powers of heaven! To you I call!

SCENE SIXTEEN

[*Enter a Greek* CAPTAIN *and Achilles' followers with his armor.*]

ACHILLES
What have you to report?

CAPTAIN
                    Leave, son of Peleus!
Our luck has turned, the winds of chance have lured
The Amazons to victory once again,
They're flying headlong to this very place,
Their battle cry is now: "Penthesilea!"

ACHILLES [*stands up and tears off his garlands*]
My weapons, bring them! And the horses, quick!
I'm going to crush them with my chariot wheels!

PENTHESILEA [*her lip quivering*]
No, look at him, the fiend! Is this the same——?

ACHILLES [*wildly*]
Are they still far away?

CAPTAIN
                    Here in the valley
You can already see their golden crescent.

ACHILLES [*putting on his armor*]
Take her away!

A GREEK
            Where to?

ACHILLES
                    To the Greek camp.
In a few moments I will follow you.

THE GREEK [*to* PENTHESILEA]
Up on your feet now, lady.

PROTHOË
                    Oh my Queen!

PENTHESILEA [*beside herself*]
No flash of lightning, Zeus, for pity's sake?

SCENE SEVENTEEN

[*Enter* ODYSSEUS *and* DIOMEDES *with the army.*]

DIOMEDES [*crossing the stage*]
Dolopian hero, leave this place! Away!
There's only one path open to you still,
And now the women are about to cut it.
So hurry, get out!

[*Exit.*]

ODYSSEUS
                Greeks, take this Queen away.
ACHILLES [*to the* CAPTAIN]
Alexis! Do me a favor. Help her rise.
THE GREEK [*to the* CAPTAIN]
She isn't moving.
ACHILLES [*to the* GREEKS *attending him*]
                Where's my shield! My lance!

[*Calling on her to rise, since she is resisting*]

Penthesilea!
PENTHESILEA
                Son of the Nereid!
You will not follow me to Themiscyra?
You will not follow me to that fair temple
That rises tall among the distant oaks?
Come here, I haven't told you everything—
ACHILLES [*fully armed now, approaching her and
offering her his hand*]
My Queen—to Phthia.
PENTHESILEA
                Oh!—To Themiscyra!

SCENE NINETEEN

[*The* HIGH PRIESTESS *of Diana with her*
PRIESTESSES, PENTHESILEA, PROTHOË,
and AMAZONS *in attendance*]

AMAZONS
Hurrah! Hurrah! Hurrah! The Queen is saved!
PENTHESILEA [*after a pause*]
A curse upon this vile, disgraceful triumph!
A curse on every tongue that celebrates it,
Accursed the air that carries the message on!
Was I not his, both by the luck of battle
And by the noble laws of chivalry?
When human beings contend among *themselves*—
In war, not in a fight with wolf or tiger:
Is there a law, I ask, by which a soldier,
After surrendering, could be released
Again from bondage to his conqueror?
—Son of the Nereid!
AMAZONS
                           Gods! Am I hearing right?
MEROË
Most venerable Priestess of Diana,
Step forward, please, I beg you.
ASTERIA
                           She is angry
Because we cut her bonds of servitude!
THE HIGH PRIESTESS [*stepping forward from the
throng of women*]
Well then, my Queen, this diatribe of yours
Does set a worthy cap, I must confess,
Upon the deeds of this unfortunate day.
Not only that, in disregard of custom,
You seek out your opponent in the field;
Not only that, failing to cast him down,

You're thrown by him instead; not only that you
Garland him with roses in return:
But you revile your loyal followers
Who broke your chains, you turn away from us,
And call the conqueror to come back to you!
Very well, then, noble daughter of Tanaïs,
I beg your pardon for this hasty act—
This rash mistake—it was no more than that.
I do feel sorry for the blood it cost us,
And from the bottom of my heart I wish
We'd kept the prisoners we lost for you.
Free, in our people's name, I now pronounce you,
And you may wend your feet wherever you please,
May run with fluttering garments after him
Who clapped you in irons, and bring back to him
The bonds we broke, for mending. As you say,
The sacred rules of war demand no less!
But we, you'll not begrudge us this, my Queen,
We shall give up this war and turn our feet
Homeward to Themiscyra once again;
For we, at any rate, can't *beg* those Greeks
Now running for their lives to stop and wait,
Nor, with the victor's wreath in hand, like you,
Implore them off their feet into the dust.

[*Pause*]

PENTHESILEA [*reeling*]
Prothoë!
  PROTHOË
   My sister heart!
  PENTHESILEA
     I beg you, stay with me.
  PROTHOË
In death, you know it——My Queen, you're trembling, why?
  PENTHESILEA
It's nothing, nothing, I'll compose myself.
  PROTHOË
A great grief struck you, Queen. Meet it with greatness.

PENTHESILEA

And they're all lost?

PROTHOË

Who lost, my precious Queen?

PENTHESILEA

That splendid company of youths we struck down?—
All lost because of me?

PROTHOË

It doesn't matter.
You'll win them for us in another war.

PENTHESILEA [on her bosom]

Oh never!

PROTHOË

What are you saying, my Queen?

PENTHESILEA

Oh never!
I want to hide in everlasting darkness!

SCENE TWENTY

[*Enter a* HERALD.]

MEROË
There comes a herald, my Queen!
ASTERIA
                              What do you want?
PENTHESILEA [*with faint joy*]
It's from Achilles! —Oh what will I hear?
Oh Prothoë, make him leave!
PROTHOË
                              What do you bring?
THE HERALD
I have been sent here by Achilles, Queen,
The reed-crowned Nereid's exalted son,
And through my mouth he sends this message to you:
Since your desire is to lead him home
A prisoner to your native meadowlands,
And he, for his part, has a keen desire
To carry you a captive home to his,
He challenges you once again to fight him
For life and death upon the field, and let
The brazen tongue of fate, the sword, decide,
Before the just tribunal of the gods,
Which one of you is worthier, you or he,
By their inviolable, sacred will,
To lick the dust at his opponent's feet.
Are you inclined to fight for such a wager?
PENTHESILEA [*turning pale for an instant*]
Your tongue be loosened by a thunderbolt,
Damned speechifier, before you talk again!
I'd just as gladly hear a sandstone block
Come hurtling down a mountain precipice,
Crashing against this wall and that, forever.

[*To* PROTHOË]

—You must repeat it for me word for word.
    PROTHOË [*trembling*]
The son of Peleus, I believe, has sent him
To challenge you to meet him in the field;
Simply refuse yourself to him, say no.
    PENTHESILEA
It is not possible.
    PROTHOË
                Why not, my Queen?
    PENTHESILEA
The son of Peleus summons me to battle?
    PROTHOË
Shall I dismiss the man and tell him no?
    PENTHESILEA
The son of Peleus summons me to battle?
    PROTHOË
To battle, yes, my mistress, so I said.
    PENTHESILEA
He knows my weakness, and would challenge me
To match his strength in battle, Prothoë?
This faithful breast leaves him unmoved until
With his sharp spear he's broken it to pieces?
Did all the words I whispered in his ear
Resound on it as vain and speechless music?
The temple in the trees means nothing to him,
My hand laid garlands on a marble statue?
    PROTHOË
Forget the unfeeling man.
    PENTHESILEA [*fervently*]
                So be it, then.
I feel the strength now to stand up to him:
I'll send him sprawling, even if the giants
And centaur-killing Lapiths come to help him!
    PROTHOË
Beloved Queen—
    MEROË
            Won't you consider first—

PENTHESILEA [*interrupting her*]
You shall have *all* our prisoners back again!

HERALD
You're willing, then, to meet——?

PENTHESILEA
                                        I'll take my stand:
Before the gods' tribunal—the Furies, too,
I call them all to witness—let him meet me!

[*Thunder*]

HIGH PRIESTESS
Penthesilea, if my words offended,
Please don't requite the pain—

PENTHESILEA
                                        Don't, holy Mother!
Your words shall not have been pronounced in vain.

MEROË
Most reverend Mother, only you can sway her—

HIGH PRIESTESS
My Queen, do you not hear the sound of his wrath?

PENTHESILEA
I call him down to me with all his thunders!

FIRST COLONEL [*agitated*]
Princesses—

SECOND COLONEL
                There is no way!

THIRD COLONEL
                                        It *can't* be——!

PENTHESILEA [*wildly*]
Come here, Ananke, leader of the dogs!

FIRST COLONEL
We are dispersed, and weakened—

SECOND COLONEL
                                        We are tired—

PENTHESILEA
You with the elephants, Thyrroë!

PROTHOË
                                        Queen!

Would you use dogs and elephants against him—
    PENTHESILEA
You sickle-bladed chariots, gleaming bright,
Prepare the harvest festival of war,
Come, row on row, my ghastly reapers, quick!
And you that thresh the crop of human corn,
That it be crushed forever, seed and stalk,
My mounted troops, assemble round about me!
Ferocious pomp of war, unmerciful,
Magnificent destroyer, on you I call!

> [*She grasps the great bow from an* AMAZON*'s hand.
> Enter* AMAZONS *with packs of dogs on leashes; later
> elephants, flaming torches, scythed chariots, etc.*]

    PROTHOË
My soul's beloved, listen to your friend!
    PENTHESILEA [*turning to the dogs*]
Up, Tigris, up, I need you! Up, Leäna!
Up, up, Melampus with your shaggy mane!
Up, Aklë, faster than the fox, up, Sphinx,
And you, Alector, who runs down the doe,
Up, Oxus, terror of the wild boar,
And fearless even of the lion, Hyrcaon!

> [*Violent peal of thunder*]

    PROTHOË
Oh! She's beside herself—!
    FIRST COLONEL
                   She is insane!
    PENTHESILEA [*kneels down, showing every sign of
madness, while the dogs set up a fearful howling*]
To thee, my god, Ares, thou terrible one,
To thee, high founder of my house, I call!
Oh!—send thy brazen carriage down to me:
Here where the walls of cities and their gates
Crumble at thy advance, destroyer god,
Who tramplest underfoot the crowd-wedged streets;

Oh!—send thy brazen carriage down to me:
That I may set my foot into its shell,
Take up the reins, fly rolling through the fields,
And like a thunderbolt from stormy clouds
Bear down on that Greek's head with all thy force!

[*She stands up.*]

FIRST COLONEL
Princesses!
SECOND COLONEL
Hurry! Prevent her! She's gone mad!
PROTHOË
Listen to me, great Queen!
PENTHESILEA [*drawing the bow*]
Here's to good sport!
Let's see whether my shaft still hits the mark.

[*She aims at* PROTHOË.]

PROTHOË [*collapsing*]
Olympians!
A PRIESTESS [*quickly moving behind* PENTHE-
SILEA]
Achilles calls!
A SECOND PRIESTESS [*doing likewise*]
The Peleid!
A THIRD PRIESTESS
Right there, behind you!
PENTHESILEA
Where?
FIRST PRIESTESS
Was that not he?
PENTHESILEA
No, no, the Furies have not gathered yet.
Ananke, follow me! All others, follow!

[*Exit* PENTHESILEA *with all the troops, accompa-
nied by violent claps of thunder.*]

MEROË [*lifting* PROTHOË *up*]
The horror!

ASTERIA
        Women! Follow her! Away!

HIGH PRIESTESS [*deathly pale*]
Eternal gods! What judgment have you passed?

SCENE TWENTY-ONE

[*Enter* ACHILLES *and* DIOMEDES. *Later* ODYSSEUS
enters, and finally the HERALD.]

ACHILLES
Now listen, Diomede, do me a favor,
Don't tell that sour, self-righteous prig, Odysseus,
A single word of what I'm going to tell you;
It bothers me, in fact it makes me ill,
To see that haughty sneer around his lip.
DIOMEDES
Did you send her the herald, Peleid?
Is it true? Really?
ACHILLES
               Let me tell you, friend:
—But you, keep quiet, do you understand?
No comment, not a word! —This wondrous woman,
Half grace, half fury, is in love with me —
And I—for all the womanhood of Greece,
By the Styx! By all of Hades!—love her too.
DIOMEDES
What!
ACHILLES
      Yes. Some whim, though, which to her is holy,
Demands that I fall captive to her sword;
And not till then can she in love embrace me.
So I sent—
DIOMEDES
          Crazy fool!
ACHILLES
              He doesn't hear me!
If all his livelong life, throughout the world,
That round blue eye of his has never seen it,
He's not equipped to grasp it with his thoughts.
DIOMEDES
You want—? No, speak! You want—?

ACHILLES [*after a pause*]
—What do I want?
What monstrous thing do I intend to do?

DIOMEDES
You mean to say you've only challenged her
In order—?

ACHILLES
Great cloud-shaking Zeus! I tell you,
She will not hurt me! Sooner would her arm
Rampage against her breast in single combat,
And shout "Hurrah!" when her heart's blood spurts forth,
Than against me! —I want for but one moon
To be compliant to her wants and needs,
One or two moons, no more: now surely this
Won't make your old, flood-sodden, ebb-chewed isthmus
Collapse into the sea! —And after that,
I'm free, as I have heard from her own lips,
Free as a deer; if then she follows me,
By Jupiter! I'd be among the blessed
If I could seat her on my father's throne!

[ODYSSEUS *enters.*]

DIOMEDES
Come over here, Odysseus, please.

ODYSSEUS
Achilles!
I hear you've called the Queen into the field;
Do you intend, with our exhausted troops,
To venture misadventure once again?

DIOMEDES
There'll be no venture, friend, no fight at all.
He plans to make himself her prisoner.

ODYSSEUS
What?

ACHILLES [*flushing violently*]
Take your face away from me, I beg you!

ODYSSEUS
He plans—

DIOMEDES
            You heard me right! To split her helmet;
Look fierce, and bluster, like a warrior;
Go pounding at her shield, make mighty sparks,
And mutely, as a man disarmed and vanquished,
Lay himself down before her dainty feet.
        ODYSSEUS
Is this man in his right mind, son of Peleus?
Did you hear what he said—
        ACHILLES [controlling himself]
                    I have to ask you
To please not curl your upper lip, Odysseus.
For, by the justice of the gods, that twitch
Infects me likewise, right down to my fist.
        ODYSSEUS [furiously]
By all the burning waters of Cocytus!
I want to know if I heard right or not!
You'd better tell me, son of Tydeus, now,
And solemnly, so I can clear this up,
Swear that what I'm about to ask is true.
He's planning to surrender to the Queen?
        DIOMEDES
You heard it!
        ODYSSEUS
            He wants to go to Themiscyra?
        DIOMEDES
True.

        ODYSSEUS
        And Helen's rescue, our great fight
Before the walls of Troy, this lunatic
Thinks he can drop it like a toy, simply
Because some other bright thing's caught his fancy?
        DIOMEDES
By Jupiter! I swear it.
        ODYSSEUS [crossing his arms]
                    I can't believe it.
        ACHILLES
He talks about the walls of Troy.

ODYSSEUS
                              What?

DIOMEDES
                                        What?

ODYSSEUS
I thought you said something.

ACHILLES
                              I?

ODYSSEUS
                              You!

ACHILLES
                              I said:

He talks about the walls of Troy.

ODYSSEUS
                              Well, yes!
I asked him, like a man possessed, if Helen
And our great fight before the walls of Troy
Have been forgotten, like a morning dream?

ACHILLES [*stepping up closer to him*]
Son of Laertes, if the walls of Troy
Should sink, you understand, so that a lake,
A bluish one, replaced the battlements;
And if at night gray fishermen attached
Their boat by moonlight to the weathercocks;
And if a pike were lord in Priam's palace,
And if in Helen's bed a pair of otters,
Or, say, a pair of water rats, embraced:
It would mean just the same to me as now.

ODYSSEUS
By the Styx! He means it, son of Tydeus!

ACHILLES
By the Styx! By the Lernaean bog! By Hades!
The upper world! The lower world! Why not?
Or any other world! Indeed, I mean it;
I want to see the temple of Diana!

ODYSSEUS [*aside to* DIOMEDES]
See that he doesn't leave this place, my friend,
If you don't mind.

DIOMEDES

If I—you must be joking!
If *you* don't mind, please lend me both your arms.

[*Enter the* HERALD.]

ACHILLES

Ha! Does she accept? Let's hear it! Does she accept?

HERALD

She does, Achilles, yes, she's on her way;
But bringing dogs as well, and elephants,
And a tremendous host of mounted troops;
Why these for single combat, I don't know.

ACHILLES

That's what she owes to custom. Fine. Now follow!
—Oh she's a sly one, by the eternal gods!
——With dogs, you say?

HERALD

Yes, sir.

ACHILLES

And elephants?

HERALD

Enough to strike cold terror in the heart!
If her intent were to attack the camp
Of the Atrides outside Troy, she couldn't look
More sinister, or come more fiercely armored.

ACHILLES [*into his beard*]
No doubt they'll eat from my hands— Follow me!
—Oh! They'll be just as tame as she.

[*Exit* ACHILLES *with his attendants.*]

DIOMEDES

He's mad!

ODYSSEUS

Let's tie him, gag him—listen, all you Greeks!

DIOMEDES

The Amazons are here already—off!

SCENE TWENTY-TWO

[*The* HIGH PRIESTESS, *her face white; several other*
PRIESTESSES *and* AMAZONS]

HIGH PRIESTESS
Go, women, fetch some ropes!
FIRST PRIESTESS
                              Your Holiness!
HIGH PRIESTESS
Take her and throw her to the ground! Bind her!
AN AMAZON
Bind whom, Your Grace? The Queen?
HIGH PRIESTESS
                              I mean that dog!
—There's no restraining her with human hands.
THE AMAZONS
Most reverend Mother! You're beside yourself.
HIGH PRIESTESS
Three maidens did she kick into the dust
Whom we had sent to stop her; Meroë,
Because she blocked her path on bended knee,
Imploring her with all the sweetest names—
She set the dogs on her and chased her off.
When, from afar, I came a few steps closer,
She stooped immediately and, with both hands,
Fixing me with a most malignant stare,
Took up a rock—I would have been destroyed
Had I not taken refuge in the crowd.
FIRST PRIESTESS
Oh this is awful!
SECOND PRIESTESS
                    It is terrible, women.
HIGH PRIESTESS
She's in a frenzy now among her dogs,

Her lips all flecked with foam, calling them sisters,
Those howling, baying brutes, and like a Maenad,
Dancing across the meadows with her bow,
She's prodding them, the murder-breathing pack,
Urging them on to catch the fairest game,
She says, that ever ranged upon the earth.
THE AMAZONS
Ye gods of Orcus! How you punish her!
HIGH PRIESTESS
Therefore, Mars' daughters, quickly with a rope,
Across those forking paths, lay out a snare,
Covered with brush, for her advancing tread.
And when her foot is caught, pull the rope tight
And drag her down just like a rabid dog;
That we may bind her, carry her back home,
And see if there's a way we still might save her.
THE AMAZON ARMY [offstage]
Hurrah! Hurrah! Hurrah! Achilles falls!
The hero has been taken prisoner!
Our Queen will decorate his head with roses!

[Pause]

HIGH PRIESTESS [her voice choked with joy]
Did I hear rightly?
PRIESTESSES AND AMAZONS
                    Praise to the gods above!
HIGH PRIESTESS
That exclamation, was it not of joy?
FIRST PRIESTESS
A shout of triumph, holy reverend Mother,
And none more blissful ever touched my ear!
HIGH PRIESTESS
Who will report to me?
SECOND PRIESTESS
                    You, Terpi! Quick!
Go mount that hill and tell us what you see!
AN AMAZON [who has climbed the hill, horrified]
On you, horrific gods of hell, I call

As witnesses—what is this that I see!

Well, now—as if she'd cast eyes on Medusa!

PRIESTESSES
What do you see? Speak out!

THE AMAZON
                            Penthesilea,
She's lying down, her grim dogs close beside her,
She who was born of human loins, tearing—
She's tearing him to pieces, limb from limb!

HIGH PRIESTESS
Oh gods! Oh horror! Horror!

ALL
                            Horrible!

THE AMAZON
The ghastly riddle has an answer, maidens.
It's coming toward us now, pale as a corpse.

[*She descends from the hill.*]

SCENE TWENTY-THREE

[*Enter* MEROË.]

MEROË
Oh holy priestesses of Artemis,
And Mars' pure daughters, listen and attend:
I am the Gorgon come of Africa,
And as you stand, my stare turns you to stone.

HIGH PRIESTESS
Speak, horrid one! What happened?

MEROË
                As you know,
She had set out to meet the youth she loves,
She who henceforth shall be unnameable,
In the bewilderment of her young senses
Arming with all the dread of weaponry
The burning wish to capture and possess him.
Dogs howling round about her, elephants
Stamping beside, she hurried, with bow in hand:
The face of War, convulsed in civil strife,
When, drenched in blood, his ghastly apparition
Goes loping through the land with strides of horror,
Whirling his torch above the flowering cities,
Is not as hideous nor as wild as hers.
Achilles, who, our soldiers all assure me,
Had challenged her to fight, the young fool, only
In order, of his own free will, to yield:
For he, too—oh how mighty are the gods!
He was in love with her, touched by her youth,
And wished to follow her to Diana's temple—
He approaches her, filled with sweet premonitions,
Alone, for he has left his friends behind.
But now that with such terror-breathing menace

But now that with such terror-breathing menace
She thunders in on him, who, unsuspecting,
Came armed, half playfully, with but a spear

She thunders in on him, who, unsuspecting,
Came armed, half playfully, with but a spear:
He stops, and turns his slender neck, and listens,
And bolts in terror, stops, and bolts again:
Almost like a young deer that, from afar,
Hears the grim lion's roar among the cliffs.
He cries: Odysseus! with constricted voice,
And shyly turns his head, cries: Diomede!
And wants to flee and still rejoin his friends;
Alas, he sees his path already cut,
Stops short, lifts up both hands, stoops, tries to take
A tree for shelter, the unfortunate man,
A dark pine tree, low-hung with heavy branches.
And all the while the Queen was drawing near,
Her pack of dogs apace behind her, scanning
The woods and towering mountains, like a hunter;
And just as he begins to part the boughs
In order to sink down before her feet:
Aha! The antlers give away the stag,
She cries, and, with the strength of madness, draws
And draws the bow until the two ends kiss,
And raises up the bow and aims and shoots,
And drives the arrow through his throat; he falls:
A yell of triumph rises from our people.
Yet he still lives, most pitiable of men,
The arrow jutting out behind his neck,
He rises, gasping, falls head over heels,
And rises once again and wants to flee;
But now "Attack!" she cries, "Tigris! Attack!
Hyrkaon! Sphinx! Attack, Melampus! Dirke!"
And throws—throws herself on him, oh Diana!
With the whole pack, and pulling at his crest,
For all the world a dog with other dogs,
One's at his breast, the other takes his neck,
She drags him down so hard it makes the ground quake!
He, crimson with his own blood, writhing, reaches
Out to her soft cheek, touches her, and cries:
Penthesilea! My bride! What are you doing?

Is this the rosy feast you promised me?
But she—a lioness would have heeded him,
However ravenous and wild for prey,
Howling her hunger through the snowy wastes—
She sinks—tearing the armor off his body—
Into his ivory breast she sinks her teeth,
She and her savage dogs in competition,
Oxus and Sphinx chewing into his right breast,
And she into his left; when I arrived,
The blood was dripping from her mouth and hands.

[*Horrified pause*]

If you have heard me, women, speak to me,
Give me a sign that you still live and breathe.

[*Pause*]

FIRST PRIESTESS [*weeping on the breast of the*
SECOND]
So fine a maiden, Hermia! So modest!
So deft at every art and handicraft!
So lovely when she danced, and when she sang!
So good a mind! Such dignity and grace!
HIGH PRIESTESS
That's not Otrerë's child, not she! The Gorgon
Spawned her somewhere behind the palace walls!
FIRST PRIESTESS [*continuing*]
She was a child as of the nightingale
That dwells about the temple of Diana.
She sat there, cradled in an oak tree's crown,
Singing away, and warbling, and singing,
All through the quiet night, till some far wanderer
Would hear, and feel his heart swell in his breast.
She would not crush or kick the mottled worm
That chanced to play beneath her hovering heel;
An arrow shot to pierce a wild boar's heart
She would call back, afraid but that his eye,

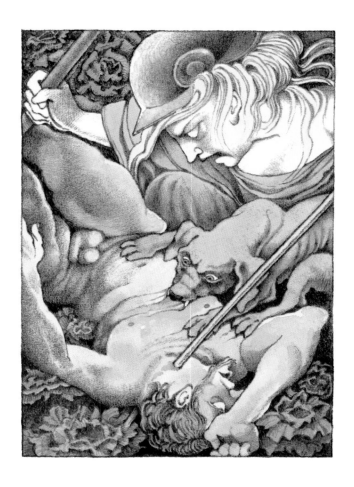

He, crimson with his own blood, writhing, reaches
Out to her soft cheek, touches her, and cries:
Penthesilea! My bride! What are you doing?
Is this the rosy feast you promised me?

Broken in death, should melt her in remorse,
And make her drop before him to her knees!

[*Pause*]

MEROË

Now she stands silent, gruesome to behold,
Beside his corpse, dogs sniffing all around her,
And stares, as if upon an empty page
—Her bow victorious slung across her shoulder—
Into the infinite without a sound.
At length we ask her, with our hair on end,
What she has done: No answer. If she knows us:
No answer. If she would follow us: No answer.
Then horror seized me and I fled to you.

SCENE TWENTY-FOUR

[PENTHESILEA. *The body of* ACHILLES, *covered with a red carpet. The* HIGH PRIESTESS, MEROË, PROTHOË, *and others.*]

FIRST AMAZON
Look, women! There she is, look! Walking toward us,
A wreath of nettles on her head, the horror,
In place of laurels, twined with barren twigs
Of hawthorn, following behind the corpse,
Her bow slung festively across her shoulder,
As if she'd killed a mortal enemy!
SECOND PRIESTESS
Oh see her hands——!
FIRST PRIESTESS
                    Oh women, turn away!
PROTHOË [*falling upon the* HIGH PRIESTESS*'s
bosom*]
Oh my Mother!
HIGH PRIESTESS
                    I call upon Diana!
I had no part in this atrocity!
FIRST AMAZON
She stands up straight before the High Priestess.
SECOND AMAZON
She makes a sign, look!
HIGH PRIESTESS
                    Go! Away, you horror!
You citizen of Hades! Off, I say!
Here, take my veil, and cover her with it.

[*She tears off her veil and throws it in the* QUEEN*'s
face.*]

FIRST AMAZON
She's like a living corpse. It doesn't move her——!

SECOND AMAZON
Still the same gesture —
THIRD AMAZON
                              Pointing over and over—
FIRST AMAZON
She's pointing at the feet of the High Priestess—
SECOND AMAZON
Look, look!
HIGH PRIESTESS
                    What do you want? Away from me!
Go to the ravens, specter! Off! Go! Rot!
Your eyes are killing all my life's content.
FIRST AMAZON
Ah, look, they understood her—
SECOND AMAZON
                                        Now she's calm.
FIRST AMAZON
They were supposed to lay the Peleid
Before the Priestess' feet, that's what she meant.
THIRD AMAZON
But why particularly at her feet?
FOURTH AMAZON
What does she mean by that?
HIGH PRIESTESS
                              What are you *after*?
Why put this *corpse* in front of me? Let it be
Covered by mountains, inaccessible,
And with it all remembrance of your deed!
You, you—you no more human, what to call you?
Did *I* exact this crime of you, this murder?—
If soft reproaches from the mouth of love
Can drive you to such butchery, then let
The Furies come and teach us gentleness!
FIRST AMAZON
She just keeps gazing at the High Priestess.
SECOND AMAZON
Straight in her face—
THIRD AMAZON
                              Unwavering and firm,

As if she meant to stare her through and through.—

HIGH PRIESTESS

Go, Prothoë, I beg you, please, go, go,
I cannot bear to look at her, remove her.

PROTHOË [*weeping*]

Oh misery!

HIGH PRIESTESS

      Resolve yourself!

PROTHOË

            What she

Has done is too revolting. Let me be.

HIGH PRIESTESS

Strength, Prothoë. —She had a lovely mother.
—Go, offer her your help and lead her off.

PROTHOË

I never want to look at her again!—

SECOND AMAZON

See, she's examining that slender arrow!

FIRST AMAZON

She turns it in her hands—

THIRD AMAZON

           She measures it!

FIRST PRIESTESS

It seems to be the shaft she used to kill him.

FIRST AMAZON

It is!

SECOND AMAZON

    Look at the way she wipes the blood off!
The way she rubs it clean of every spot!

THIRD AMAZON

I wonder what she's thinking.

SECOND AMAZON

          And the feathers,
The way she dries them, ruffles, teases them!
So neatly! Everything just as it should be.
Oh look at her!

THIRD AMAZON

      —Is this her usual custom?

FIRST AMAZON
To do this for herself?
FIRST PRIESTESS
                    Her bow and arrows,
She always cared for them with her own hands.
SECOND PRIESTESS
Oh yes, she held them sacred, that's the truth!——
SECOND AMAZON
But now she takes the quiver from her shoulder
And puts the arrow back into its place.
THIRD AMAZON
Now she is finished—
SECOND AMAZON
                    Now it is all done —
FIRST PRIESTESS
Now once again she looks out on the world—!
SEVERAL WOMEN
Oh miserable sight! Oh desolate
Like desert sand that yields no blade of grass!
A pleasure garden struck by fiery streams
Boiled in the innards of the earth and then
Spewed out upon the blossoms of its breast,
Is handsomer to look at than her face.

[PENTHESILEA *shudders violently; she drops the bow.*]

HIGH PRIESTESS
Oh the abomination!
PROTHOË [*frightened*]
                    Now what is it?
FIRST AMAZON
The bow is falling, falling from her hands!
SECOND AMAZON
Look how it totters—
FOURTH AMAZON
                    Clangs, and sways, and drops—!
SECOND AMAZON
And shudders one more time upon the ground—

133

THIRD AMAZON
And dies—as it was born to Queen Tanaïs.

[*Pause*]

HIGH PRIESTESS [*suddenly turning to* PENTHE-
SILEA]
Oh my great Queen and mistress, please forgive me!
Well pleased is Artemis, the goddess, with you,
Your deed has put her anger back to rest.
The mighty founder of our women's state,
Tanaïs herself, I will admit it now,
Wielded the bow no worthier than you.
FIRST AMAZON
She's silent—
SECOND AMAZON
                      Her eyes are filling—
THIRD AMAZON
                                      She lifts her finger,
All stained with blood, what does she— Look, oh look!
SECOND AMAZON
Oh sight more cutting to the heart than knives!
FIRST AMAZON
She wipes a tear away.
HIGH PRIESTESS [*falling on* PROTHOË*'s breast*]
                      Oh Artemis!
Oh what a tear!
FIRST PRIESTESS
                      A tear, most holy Mother,
That silent steals into the human breast,
And pulls on all the fire bells of emotion
And cries out: Misery! until the whole
Race, roused from sleep, comes pouring from the eyes
To gather into lakes of lamentation
Around the ruin of her soul and weep.
HIGH PRIESTESS [*with a bitter expression*]
Well, then—if Prothoë will not assist her,
She'll have to die here in her pain alone.

PROTHOË [*Her features express the most violent struggle. Thereupon, approaching* PENTHESILEA, *she speaks, her voice broken by sobs.*]
Will you not sit with me a while, my Queen?
Will you not rest upon my faithful bosom?
Much have you struggled, on this day of terror,
And greatly, greatly suffered—from so much suffering
Would you not rest upon my faithful bosom?

[PENTHESILEA *looks around as if for a chair.*]

PROTHOË
Go fetch a seat for her! You see she wants one.

[*The* AMAZONS *roll up a stone.* PENTHESILEA *sits down, supported by* PROTHOË. *Then* PROTHOË *sits down herself.*]

PROTHOË
You know me, don't you, sister heart?

[PENTHESILEA *looks at her, her face brightening a little.*]

PROTHOË
                                        I am
Your friend, who loves you, Prothoë.

[PENTHESILEA *gently strokes her cheek.*]

PROTHOË
                                Oh you
To whom my heart bows down on bended knee,
How you move me!

[*She kisses the* QUEEN*'s hand.*]

                        You must be very tired.

Ah, how your trade is writ all over you!
Well—victory's not come by neat and clean,
And every workshop makes its master's garment.
But how about your washing yourself now,
Your hands and face? —Shall I fetch you some water?
——Beloved Queen!

[PENTHESILEA *looks down at herself and nods.*]

PROTHOË
            All right. She wants me to.

[*She motions to the* AMAZONS, *who go to fetch water.*]

—It will be good for you, it will refresh you,
And gently, stretched upon a carpet, cool,
You shall recover from this hard day's labor.
      FIRST PRIESTESS
But if you sprinkle her with water, watch out,
She may remember.
      HIGH PRIESTESS
                Why, I trust she will.
      PROTHOË
You *trust* she will, Your Holiness? —I fear it.
      HIGH PRIESTESS [*apparently pondering something*]
But why? How so? —It's just that we can't risk it,
Or else the body of Achilles should—

[PENTHESILEA *shoots a furious glance at the* HIGH
PRIESTESS.]

      PROTHOË
Don't! Don't—!
      HIGH PRIESTESS
            No, no, my Queen, it's nothing, nothing!
You shall have everything just as it is.—
      PROTHOË
Take off your victor's wreath, your thorny laurels,
We're all aware you are the conqueror.

And open up your collar— There, that's good!
Why, look! I see a wound, and deep! Poor dear!
You haven't had an easy time at all—
But now your triumph's all the greater for it!
—Oh Artemis!

[*Two* AMAZONS *bring a large shallow marble basin with water.*]

PROTHOË
                    Here! Set the basin down.—
What do you say now, shall I wet your head?
And it won't frighten you———? What are you doing?

[PENTHESILEA *drops down from her seat onto her knees in front of the basin and pours water over her head.*]

PROTHOË
Look here! You seem to be quite hale, my Queen!
—Do you feel better now?
            PENTHESILEA [*looking around*]
                    Ah, Prothoë!

[*She pours water over herself again.*]

MEROË [*joyfully*]
She speaks!
            HIGH PRIESTESS
                    Praise to the gods above!
            PROTHOË
                            Good, good!
            MEROË
She's coming back to life!
            PROTHOË
                    That's excellent!
All the way under with your head, like that!
Again, my love! Like that! Like a young swan!—
            MEROË
How lovely, look!

FIRST PRIESTESS
                    The way she hangs her head!
MEROË
The way she lets the water trickle down!
PROTHOË
—Is that enough now?
PENTHESILEA
                    Ah!— How wonderful.
PROTHOË
Then we must put you back into your seat!—
Hand me your veils now, quick, you priestesses,
That I may dry her soaked and dripping locks!
Yours, Phania! Terpe, yours! Come, help me, sisters!
Let's cover up her head and neck completely!
Like that, and that! —And now, back to your seat!

[*She covers the* QUEEN*'s head, lifts her onto the seat,
and embraces her tightly.*]

PENTHESILEA
What is this feeling?
PROTHOË
                    Good, I should think—or not?
PENTHESILEA [*softly*]
Delicious!
PROTHOË
          Sister heart! My sweet! My life!
PENTHESILEA
Oh tell me! —Am I in Elysium?
Are you one of those nymphs forever young
That tend and wait upon our exalted Queen
When she descends, among soft murmurings
Of shady oaks, into her crystal grotto?
These features, tell me, was it just to please me
That you took on the features of my Prothoë?
PROTHOË
Oh no, my dearest Queen, not so, not so.
It is myself, your Prothoë, who holds
You in her arms, and what you see about you

Is still the world, still the same brittle world
On which the gods look down but from afar.
PENTHESILEA
I see. That's good. Truly quite good. No matter.
PROTHOË
What is it, my dear Queen?
PENTHESILEA
                                    I'm in good spirits.
PROTHOË
Explain, my love. We cannot understand—
PENTHESILEA
I'm glad that I still am. Now let me rest.

[*Pause*]

MEROË
How strange!
HIGH PRIESTESS
                    How truly wonderful a turn!
MEROË
If we could skillfully elicit from her—?
PROTHOË
—What do you think gave rise to the delusion
That you had passed into the realm of shades?
PENTHESILEA [*after a pause, in a kind of rapture*]
I feel such bliss, my sister! More than bliss!
I feel completely ripe for death— Diana!
I do not know what happened to me here,
Yet I could die this moment and believe
That I had overcome the son of Peleus.
PROTHOË [*covertly to the* HIGH PRIESTESS]
Remove the body, quick!
PENTHESILEA [*sitting up with eager interest*]
                            Oh Prothoë!
Whom are you talking to?
PROTHOË [*since the two bearers are still hesitant*]
                            Move!
PENTHESILEA
                        Oh Diana!

It's true, then, is it?

PROTHOË

        True? What true, beloved?

—Here! Gather close together!

[*She motions to the* PRIESTESSES *to hide the corpse with their bodies as it is lifted up.*]

PENTHESILEA [*joyfully holding her hands in front of her face*]

        Holy gods!

I do not have the heart to turn and look.

PROTHOË

What do you have in mind? What are you thinking?

PENTHESILEA [*looking around*]

Oh love, you are pretending.

PROTHOË

        No, by Zeus,

The world's eternal god!

PENTHESILEA [*with growing impatience*]

        Most holy maidens,

Please stand aside!

HIGH PRIESTESS [*pressing close together with the other women*]

        Beloved Queen!

PENTHESILEA [*standing up*]

        Why not?

Oh Artemis! Why shouldn't I? It's not

The first time that he stands behind my back.

MEROË

Look! How she's gripped by horror!

PENTHESILEA [*to the* AMAZONS *who are carrying the body*]

        Stop right there!—

What are you carrying? Stand! I want to know.

[*She pushes through the women until she reaches the body.*]

PROTHOË

Oh no, my Queen! Do not look any further!

PENTHESILEA

Is it he, maidens? Is it?

A CARRIER [*as the body is put down*]

Who, my Queen?

PENTHESILEA

It's not impossible, no, I can see that.
I may shoot down a swallow on the wing
And heal it afterward, so it can fly;
The stag, I lure him to my park with arrows.
But archery's a traitor to its master;
Aim but to shoot straight at the heart of fortune,
And cunningly the gods misguide your hand.
—Speak, women, did I strike too close? Is it he?

PROTHOË

Oh by the terrible powers of Olympus,
Don't ask me that!

PENTHESILEA

Away! And if his wound
Yawned wider than the jaws of Hades, still:
I want to see him!

[*She lifts the rug.*]

Which one of you committed this, you monsters!

PROTHOË

How can you ask?

PENTHESILEA

Oh holy Artemis!
Now there's no hope left for your child!

HIGH PRIESTESS

She's falling down!

PROTHOË

By all the deathless gods!
Why did you not pay heed to my advice?
You would have been more fortunate, poor soul,
To roam about in exile from the light
Of reason, on and on and on, than cast

Eyes on the horrors of this dreadful day!
—Beloved, sweetheart, hear me, please!

HIGH PRIESTESS

My Queen!

MEROË

Ten thousand hearts are here to share your pain!

HIGH PRIESTESS

Raise yourself up!

PENTHESILEA [half rising]

Oh gods, these bloody roses!
Oh gods, this wreath of wounds around his head!
These buds, all drifting downward with the scent
Of fresh-turned graves, to make the worms a feast!

PROTHOË [tenderly]

Yet it was love that wove this garland for him?

MEROË

Alas, too firmly—!

PROTHOË

And with the roses, thorns,
For sheer impatience that it be forever.

HIGH PRIESTESS

Now leave this place!

PENTHESILEA

But this I want to know,
Who courted him with such unholy zeal!—
I do not ask who put the living man
To death; by all our everlasting gods!
Free as a bird she may depart from me.
I ask who murdered him when he was dead,
And to this question answer, Prothoë.

PROTHOË

How do you mean, my Sovereign?

PENTHESILEA

I'll explain:
I do not care to know who robbed his breast
Of its Promethean spark; I do not care
Because I do not care; call it a whim:
She shall receive a pardon, she may flee.
But, Prothoë, whoever in this theft

So foully scorned the open gate and broke
Through every snow-white alabaster wall
Into this temple; whoever wreaked such havoc
Upon this youth, the likeness of the gods,
That life and putrefaction won't dispute
Possession of him; whoever ruined him so
That pity will not weep for him, that love,
Immortal love, must, like a harlot, turn
Away from him, unfaithful unto death:
On her I shall inflict my vengeance. Speak!

    PROTHOË [*to the* HIGH PRIESTESS]
What answer should one give to this delusion?

    PENTHESILEA
Well, am I going to hear it?

    MEROË
                        —Oh my Queen,
If it bring any comfort to your pain,
Inflict your vengeance on whomever you will.
Here we all stand and offer up our lives.

    PENTHESILEA
Just watch, next thing they'll claim is that *I* did it.

    HIGH PRIESTESS [*shyly*]
Who would it be, unhappy child, except—

    PENTHESILEA
Princess of hell dressed up in robes of light,
You dare tell me—?

    HIGH PRIESTESS
                  Diana be my witness!
Let this whole company surrounding you
Confirm my words! It was your arrow pierced him,
And gods in heaven! Would it were just your arrow!
But as he fell down, you, in the derangement
Of your wild senses, threw yourself upon him,
You and your pack of dogs together, and sank—
Oh my lip trembles to pronounce the word
For what you did. Don't ask! Come, let us go.

    PENTHESILEA
I need to hear it from my Prothoë first.

PROTHOË
My Queen! Don't put this question to me, please.
PENTHESILEA
What! I? You mean I—him? —Beneath my dogs—?
You mean that, with these hands, these little hands—?
And with this mouth, these lips that swell with love—?
Oh made for such a different service than—!
They helped each other, spurred each other on,
Mouth first and hand, and hand and mouth again—?
PROTHOË
My Queen! My Queen!
HIGH PRIESTESS
                              I cry out, Woe unto you!
PENTHESILEA
No, hear me, this you won't make me believe!
And were it scrawled with fire into the night,
And were the voice of thunder to proclaim it,
I'd still shout back at both of them: You lie!
MEROË
Let this faith stand, like mountains, undeterred.
It is not we who will unsettle it.
PENTHESILEA
—Why did he not defend himself at all?
HIGH PRIESTESS
He loved you, wretched creature! All he wanted
Was to surrender, that was why he came!
That was the reason why he challenged you!
He came with nothing in his heart but peace:
You could have led him to Diana's temple.
But you—
PENTHESILEA
            I see—
HIGH PRIESTESS
                        You struck—
PENTHESILEA
                              —Tore him apart.
PROTHOË
My Queen!

PENTHESILEA
    Or did it happen differently——?

MEROË
The monster!

PENTHESILEA
    Did I kiss him to death?

HIGH PRIESTESS
                Oh Heaven!

PENTHESILEA
No? Didn't kiss him? Really tore him? Speak?

HIGH PRIESTESS
Woe unto you! Go hide yourself away!
Let everlasting midnight cover you!

PENTHESILEA
——So it was a mistake. A kiss, a bite,
The two should rhyme, for one who truly loves
With all her heart can easily mistake them.

MEROË
Help her, eternal gods!

PROTHOË [*seizing the* QUEEN]
            Away!

PENTHESILEA
        Don't, don't!

[*She disengages herself and kneels in front of the body.*]

Most pitiful of mortals, you forgive me!
By Artemis, my tongue pronounced one word
For sheer unbridled haste to say another;
But now I'll tell you clearly what I meant:
This, my beloved, just this, and nothing else.

[*She kisses him.*]

HIGH PRIESTESS
Take her away!

MEROË
      This is no place for her!

PENTHESILEA
How many a maid will say, her arms wrapped round

Her lover's neck: I love you, oh so much
That if I could, I'd eat you up right here;
And later, taken by her word, the fool!
She's had enough and now she's sick of him.
You see, my love, that never was my way.
Look: When *my* arms were wrapped around your neck,
I did what I had spoken, word for word;
I was not quite so mad as it might seem.

MEROË

The monstrous woman! What was that she said?

HIGH PRIESTESS

Seize her! Take her away!

PROTHOË

                    Come now, my Queen!

PENTHESILEA [*allowing* PROTHOË *to help her up*]
All right. I'm here already.

HIGH PRIESTESS

                    You'll follow us?

PENTHESILEA

Not you!——
You go to Themiscyra, and be happy,
If you can—
Especially my Prothoë—
All of you—
And————a word in secret now, let no one hear it,
Scatter Tanaïs' ashes in the air!

PROTHOË

And you, my precious sister heart?

PENTHESILEA

I?

PROTHOË

    You!

PENTHESILEA

        —Yes, I will tell you, Prothoë.
I hereby disavow the law of women
And I shall follow him, this youth.

PROTHOË

How do you mean, my Queen?

HIGH PRIESTESS

Unhappy soul!

PROTHOË

You want—?

HIGH PRIESTESS

You think—

PENTHESILEA

What? Yes, I do!

MEROË

Oh Heaven!

PROTHOË

Then let me say a word, my sister heart—

[*She tries to take her dagger away.*]

PENTHESILEA

What is it? What?———You're pulling at my belt!
—I see. Right, wait! I didn't understand you.
———Here is the dagger.

[*She takes the dagger from her belt and gives it to* PRO-
THOË.]

You want the arrows too?

[*She takes the quiver from her shoulder.*]

I'll pour out the whole quiver for you—there!

[*She spills the arrows out in front of her.*]

It would be sweet, though, on the one hand—

[*She picks up several arrows.*]

For this one here—or not? Or was it this one—?
Yes, this one! Right— But never mind! There! Take them!
Take all the arrows, keep them!

[*She gathers up the whole bundle of arrows and puts them in* PROTHOË*'s hands.*]

PROTHOË

Hand them over.

PENTHESILEA

For now I shall descend into my breast,
And dig a shaft, and quarry out the cold
Ore of a feeling that annihilates.
This ore I purify in fire of grief
To hardest steel; in poison then, of bitter,
Burning remorse, I soak it, through and through;
Now carry it toward Hope's eternal anvil,
And grind and sharpen it into a dagger;
And to this dagger now I yield my breast:
So! So! So! So! Again! —Now it is done.

[*She falls and dies.*]

PROTHOË [*lifting the* QUEEN]
She's dying!

MEROË

She follows him indeed!

PROTHOË

May she fare well!
For her there was no further staying here.

[*She lays her on the ground.*]

HIGH PRIESTESS

Oh gods! How fragile is this humankind!
How proudly she, who now lies snapped, stood rooted
High on the peaks of life just hours ago!

PROTHOË

Because she flowered with too much pride and spirit,
She fell. The dead oak stands against the storm,
The healthy one he topples with a crash
Because his grasp can reach into its crown.

148

Oh gods! How fragile is this humankind!
How proudly she, who now lies snapped, stood rooted
High on the peaks of life just hours ago!

NOTES

[The following notes are partly based on the excellent scholarly appendices in the Reclam and the Bibliothek Deutscher Klassiker editions of Penthesilea.]

SCENE ONE

page

5. *Jupiter, Mars:* From the outset, and throughout the play, Kleist ignores the distinction between the names of the Greek and the Roman gods and interchanges them freely.

   Agamemnon: The leader of the Greek forces in the Trojan War.

   Myrmidons: A Thessalian tribe that fought by the side of the Greeks in the war against Troy. Their leader was Achilles.

   Deiphobus: One of the sons of King Priam of Troy (hence "Priamid"), he assumed leadership of his people's army after the death of Hector, his brother.

   Ilium: Latin for Ilion. The city of Troy was named after Ilos, the son of Tros, the Trojans' eponymous hero.

6. *Styx:* Along with Acheron and Cocytos, the Styx was one of three rivers surrounding the underworld.

7. *Peleus' son:* Achilles was the son of Peleus, King of the Myrmidons in Thessalía.

   Argives: Inhabitants of the city of Argos and the region of Argolis in the Peloponnisos. The term was used by Homer interchangeably with "Danaeans" to mean all the peoples of Greece.

8. *Danaeans:* Greeks; the name goes back to Danaus, the founder and King of Argos.

   Furies: Gk. Erinnyes or Eumenides: goddesses of retribution, created by Gaia, the earth goddess, out of drops of blood she collected from the mutilated body of Uranos after he was castrated by his son, Chronos.

9. *Helen's capture:* The abduction of Menelaos' wife, Helen, by Paris, the son of King Priam of Troy, set off the Trojan War.

   Etolia: Diomedes is King of Etolia.

10. *the son of Thetis:* Achilles' mother was the nymph Thetis.
   Orcus: Underworld; Gk. Tartaros.
11. *son of Atreus:* Agamemnon.
   Laertes' son: Odysseus himself.

SCENE TWO

13. *the walls of Pergamos:* Pergamos is the name of the Trojan citadel.
14. *Isthmian art:* The Isthmian games, held yearly on the isthmus of Corinth, were famous especially for their chariot races.
   son of gods: Thetis, Achilles' mother, was immortal.
16. *Hephaestos:* The god of fire and handicrafts. In his forge, he created the weapons of Achilles and also Apollo's chariot of the sun.
17. *the Atrides' wrath:* The Atrides are the sons of Atreus, Agamemnon and Menelaos.

SCENE FOUR

25. *hero of Aegina:* Achilles' father, Peleus, grew up on the island of Aegina.
   Son of the Nereid: Achilles' mother, Thetis, was one of the fifty daughters of the sea god Nereus.
26. *Dolopian hero:* Like the Dolopians, Achilles comes from Thessaly.
   sons of Atreus: Agamemnon and Menelaos.

SCENE FIVE

32. *no breast to live in:* According to legend, the Amazons had their right breast amputated immediately after birth, to make them fit for using bows and arrows later.
   ill-tempered child: Reporting to his sister Ulrike about his failure to complete *Robert Guiskard*, Kleist wrote: "Heaven denies me fame, the greatest of all earthly goods; I am throwing all the others after it, like an ill-humored child."
33. *Themiscyra:* The capital of the Amazon Empire.

39. *blessed souls:* In Greek mythology, human beings beloved by the gods were granted eternal life in a carefree, heaven-like realm called Elysium.

SCENE SIX

42. *Gorgon shield:* The Gorgon Medusa's severed head on the shield of the goddess Athena was said to strike paralyzing fear into her enemies.

SCENE SEVEN

49. *diamond belt:* The belt of the Amazon Queen Hippolyta. It was one of the twelve tasks of Hercules to steal this belt.

SCENE NINE

54. *sickles on the cars:* In Middle Eastern countries, Persia in particular, sharp blades were attached to the shafts and wheels of war chariots to protect against attacks by foot soldiers with battle-axes.

56. *Oh Aphrodite!* Significantly, Penthesilea calls on the goddess of love instead of Artemis, her tribe's protecting deity. Aphrodite was on the side of the Trojans in their war with Greece. Thus Penthesilea is invoking a powerful enemy of Achilles.

60. *Pharsos:* A city of Kleist's invention.

61. *Dardanians:* The Trojans; i.e., the descendants of Dardanus, the mythical founder of Troy.

62. *If the whole weight / Of hell bears down upon you:* In a letter to a friend on April 10, 1804, Wieland reported saying to Kleist: "Nothing is impossible to the genius of the sacred muse that accompanies you, you must complete your Guiskard, even if the entire Caucasus and Atlas should press down upon you."

63. *To roll the Ida Mountains up Mount Ossa:* The Ida is a mountain range on the island of Crete; Ossa is a mountain in Thessaly. In Greek legend, the giants Otos and Ephialtes rolled Mount Pelion on top of Mount Ossa in an attempt to storm the

seat of the gods. Penthesilea intends to outdo them by pulling Helios, the sun god—with whom she has identified Achilles—down to earth by his golden hair.

64. *Helios:* The Greek sun god, sometimes identified with Phoebus Apollo, who circles the earth in his solar chariot.

65. PRIESTESS *on the hill:* This refers back to "A PRIESTESS *on the hill*" on p. 57.

SCENE TWELVE

72. *He leaves this place / A shadow:* He will be dead, and therefore destined for Orcus, the realm of shades.

SCENE THIRTEEN

76. *unto the Pillars of Hercules:* The mountains on both sides of the Strait of Gibraltar, which for the ancients marked the end of the world. One of Hercules' tasks was to venture beyond the strait and bring back the golden apples of the Hesperides. To accomplish the deed, he bore Atlas' burden until the titan returned with the treasure. The Herculean reference recalls Wieland's exhortation after hearing sections of *Robert Guiskard* (see note to p. 62).

Her soul cannot be reckoned with: I.e., she is not calculable; the movements of her soul are enigmatic, "not fashioned for the light of day" (p. 75). Therefore any attempt to manipulate her is fraught with risk. This applies as well to Prothoë's calculation.

SCENE FOURTEEN

77. *oh dreamer!* The illusory victory scene that follows is a dream play staged by Prothoë in which Achilles pretends to have been vanquished. His pretense is false only in appearance, since Penthesilea's dream of happiness is also his own. The dream play can continue only for so long as Penthesilea is convinced that the real defeat she has suffered was "just a dream" (p. 79).

79. *just a dream . . . Could it be real?* At the moment when Penthe-

silea is in danger of realizing that her nightmare was a real event, Achilles enters the scene prepared by Prothoë, in order to play in reality what can only remain a dream.

80. *He was disarmed—weren't you?* A cue for Achilles: the fiction is a metaphoric play on words which Penthesilea can receive only in a literal sense. Viz. p. 67: "And as a man disarmed, in every sense"; and earlier on this page, "In every nobler sense, exalted Queen, / Prepared henceforth to flutter out my life / A captive bound and fettered by your eyes."

young god with roses in your cheeks: The epithet is reminiscent of Homer's description of Eos, the goddess of dawn, in the *Odyssey* (v. 121). Eos is the sister of the sun god Helios. This is the first time Penthesilea addresses Achilles in directly mythological terms as a representative of the solar principle.

81. *the sons of Inachos:* Inachos was the first King of Argos. The captured Greeks Penthesilea is referring to are only in a figurative sense his descendants.

82. *Eumenides:* The Furies, or Erinnyes, were sometimes euphemistically called the Eumenides ("the well-meaning ones").

85. *Hymen:* The god of weddings. His image was that of a handsome young man, decorated with a wreath of roses, a torch in his right hand and a veil in his left.

SCENE FIFTEEN

87. *Love, being but a small wingèd boy:* Eros (Amor or Cupid in Roman mythology) is the winged boy with the bow and arrow, a personification of love.

88. *Thallo and Carpo:* Two of the Twelve Hours, assistants of Eos in ushering in the dawn.

Hephaestos: See note for p. 16.

92. *nightingale-enchanted:* For this happy solution to the problem of translating the otherwise unreproducible *"Nachtigall-durchschmettert"* I am indebted to Martin Greenberg's version of *Penthesilea* (1989). Further down on this page, I felt constrained to borrow as well his "flower-embosomed" (for *"frucht-umblühten"*) Caucasus. I don't believe a closer approximation can be found.

92–94. *Where now the Amazonian nation rules / . . . / And then the crown was set upon her head:* Kleist combines the myth of the Amazons with that of the Danaïds, the fifty daughters of Danaus. They were expected to marry the fifty sons of Danaus' brother. On the wedding night, the women killed all the men with daggers.

93. *women's state:* The notion of a sovereign women's state with its own constitution was distinctly provocative in Kleist's time. Just a few years earlier, in 1793, Olympe de Gouges had been executed by the Jacobins for her militant advocacy of women's suffrage; also, Mary Wollstonecraft's *Vindication of the Rights of Women* (1792) had met with violent attacks in the press.

94. *The Amazons, that is, the Bosomless:* An etymological derivation from the Greek *mazos*, "breast."

96. *Deucalion:* Like the biblical Noah, Deucalion was saved from a great flood visited upon humanity by a wrathful Zeus. He asked the god to re-create humanity after the catastrophe. Zeus thereupon told him and his wife to pick up stones and throw them over their shoulders. Deucalion's stones turned into infant boys, his wife's into girls.

after yearly calculations: The annual census suggests a thoroughly rationalized system, in sharp contrast to Penthesilea's uncalculable nature: "Her soul cannot be reckoned with . . ." (p. 76).

If you had come down from the moon to meet me: Twice, earlier, Achilles has described Penthesilea as a sunlike apparition (viz. pp. 88–89: *"Oh you who come to me, a dazzling vision / Descended from above as from the realms / Of ether . . ."* and p. 91: *"How is it, wondrous woman, that, like Pallas, / . . . / You should fall suddenly as from a cloud . . ."*). This is the first time he associates Penthesilea with the moon.

97. *as his proxy:* After the murder of Vexoris, the conquering tyrant, "Mars in his stead carried out the marriage rite" (p. 93). The god has since then been considered the father of the Amazons. However, he too needs a "proxy" to wed an Amazon in his stead (see p. 99: "It happened that no substitute before / Was chosen who so pleased the brides of Mars / As the Hellenic tribes that battled there").

like a fire-blazing storm, we . . . whirl about: Kleist uses an old

German word, *Windsbraut*, literally "wind-bride"; i.e., a female personification of a whirlwind.

99. *twenty times / And three:* I.e., Penthesilea is twenty-three years old.

the deeds of that heroic war: The account follows that of Homer's *Iliad*.

102. *A day-star . . . thundering down / From Mount Olympus . . . :* Once again, Achilles is identified with Helios.

Elysium: The realm of the blessed in the underworld.

103. *Prometheus:* He created human beings out of earth and water. To animate them, he stole the celestial fire and thereby incurred the wrath of the gods, who punished him by chaining him to the Caucasus.

Phthia: Capital of the Myrmidons in southern Thessaly. Achilles is, like his father, Peleus, before him, King of the Myrmidons.

SCENE SIXTEEN

105. *their golden crescent:* The Amazons worship Artemis, goddess of the hunt and the moon. Their ensign is another indication of Penthesilea's symbolic identification with the moon.

SCENE SEVENTEEN

106. *Dolopian hero:* As on p. 26: Achilles.

SCENE TWENTY

113. *Lapiths:* A Thessalian race that drove the Centaurs out of that country. Note that Penthesilea was, earlier (p. 8 and p. 27), characterized as a "centauress."

115. *Tigris . . . Hyrcaon:* Several of these dogs' names are taken from accounts of the myth of Actaeon, who made the mistake of spying on Artemis and her nymphs as they were bathing. The goddess changed him into a stag and, with his own pack of fifty hounds, tore him to pieces.

120. *Cocytus:* One of the three rivers of the underworld.

son of Tydeus: Diomedes.

121. *Lernaean bog:* Hydra, the nine-headed serpent Hercules had to kill, lived in a bog near Lerna in the land of Argolis.

SCENE TWENTY-TWO

124. *Maenad:* The Maenads (Greek *mainades*, "the raving ones") were the Bacchae, women under the thrall of the god Dionysus who wandered about dressed in deerskins, their hair disheveled, and in their ecstasies tore animals to pieces with their teeth. Euripides' *The Bacchae* describes the dismemberment of King Pentheus by his own mother in gruesome detail.

SCENE TWENTY-THREE

126. *Gorgon come of Africa:* Medusa (see note to p. 42). The Greek historians Diodorus and Pausanias considered the Gorgons to be warlike women from Africa.

127. *A tree for shelter . . . / A dark pine tree:* A reference to the myth of King Pentheus, who hid in a pine tree to watch the Bacchae's revelries (similar to Actaeon, who secretly watched Artemis bathing with her nymphs). The women, led by the King's mother, Agave, tore him to pieces.

stag: See note for p. 115.

SCENE TWENTY-FOUR

134. *And dies—as it was born:* See the description on page 95 of the ambiguous sign that marked the founding of the women's state. The Amazon "reading" the repetition of the sign is in effect announcing the death of the Amazon nation. The High Priestess immediately counters this prophecy with another interpretation: Penthesilea has fulfilled the law.

until the whole . . . and weep: There is a similar passage in a letter Kleist wrote to his friend Ernst von Pfuel in January 1808.

"What shall I do, dear Pfuel, with all these tears? I would like
. . . to hollow out a grave with them as they drop, minute by
minute, to bury myself and you and our infinite pain . . . Pre-
serve the ruins of your soul, they will remind us forever with
joy of the romantic time of our life."

135. *To whom my heart bows down on bended knee:* In the letter
to Goethe accompanying the first issue of *Phöbus*, containing
sections from *Penthesilea* (see the Introduction to this
book, p. xviii), Kleist cited the apocryphal *Oratio Manassae*
(ca. A.D. 70): "et nun flecto genua cordis" (and now I bend the
knees of my heart).

138. *Am I in Elysium?* . . . *grotto:* Penthesilea imagines Elysium as
the place where Artemis, "our exalted Queen . . . descends . . .
into her crystal grotto" with her eternally youthful nymphs;
i.e., the paradisal place and time before Actaeon set eyes on the
goddess and was punished by being torn to pieces by his dogs.

145. *A kiss, a bite, / The two should rhyme:* In German, the words
Küsse and *Bisse* (kisses and bites) actually rhyme, and Penthesilea hopes to find justification in this coincidence.